COLLEEN
CROSS

BLOWOUT

A KATERINA CARTER FRAUD THRILLER

Copyright

BLOWOUT
A Katerina Carter Fraud Thriller

International mysteries, legal crime mystery thriller cozy mysteries police procedurals, female lead sleuth women amateur sleuths private investigators, girl, mystery books, suspense thrillers and mysteries best sellers, dragon tattoo, gone, female detectives

ISBN: 978-0-9948462-3-5 eBook

ISBN: 978-0-9948462-4-2 Paperback

Published by Slice Publishing

Blowout: A Katerina Carter Fraud Thriller

Sometimes the past is better left buried…

Fraud investigator Katerina Carter's trip to an isolated island uncovers a mysterious 1930's cult, secret passages and rumors of golden treasure. The Aquarian Foundation's arcane secrets are lost in the sands of time, but a sinister crime lies deep underwater.

Kat uncovers a horrifying truth, one the killer will protect at any cost. Exposing the secret will make the murderer strike again, and only she can stop the killer. If she's lucky she'll escape alive, but has her luck already run out?

A riveting psychological and legal thriller you'll want to read with the lights on!

Also By Colleen Cross

Katerina Carter Fraud Thriller Series

Exit Strategy

Game Theory

Blowout

Katerina Carter Color of Mystery Series

Red Handed

Blue Moon

Greenwash

Nonfiction

Anatomy of a Ponzi: Scams Past and Present

BLOWOUT

A KATERINA CARTER FRAUD THRILLER

Chapter 1

Frank sat in the cabin and looked back at the boat's wake. The day was perfect. Sunshine, a stiff breeze and hardly any marine traffic made for a perfect crossing as they headed across Georgia Strait for Vancouver Island. A perfect day for a new start. After months of preparation, the end was finally in sight.

He stole a glance at Melinda, who suntanned on the deck. She was sprawled face-down on her beach towel. Her dimpled, pasty white thighs contrasted starkly with her sunburnt back that almost blended in with her red shorts. She was motionless, either passed out or oblivious. He wasn't sure which.

She looked hideous with the burn or without it, but that hardly mattered anymore. She had really let herself go after Emily's birth, and even refused to exercise or diet. He couldn't even remember the last time he saw her in shorts. She usually wore baggy t-shirts, sweat pants, and no makeup, which was, quite frankly, an improvement over the shorts. The woman he married seven years ago was a slob with no desire to please him. Enough was enough.

His situation was intolerable because of her selfishness. She had forced him to act. Too bad it had come to this, but that was her fault. He had planned for months. Now he only had to execute his plan.

Life was about to get a whole lot better. He smiled as he imagined tomorrow. The possibilities were endless.

He actually still liked Melinda, something that surprised him. As a wife she had a lot of shortcomings and he deserved more. But could he really go through with it? Of course he could. If he didn't, he had no one to blame but himself for his miserable existence. He wasn't about to play that game. All he had to do was stick to the script and execute his plan.

Only weak people acted on their feelings, something that amused him endlessly. Most people let their emotions rule their thoughts and actions. It made for poor decisions, and it made them easy targets, too. He was no prisoner to his emotions. He was a master of logic, controller of his own destiny. He knew better than most how and when to move on. He had almost resigned himself to a wasted life, but he'd finally seen the light. He had married the old Melinda, not this frumpy version. It was time for a change, a permanent one. No messy divorce or child custody battles. If only she had paid more attention to him and not forced him to act. A few hours from now she wouldn't feel a thing.

Melinda had been his second choice on the dating site. The pickings were slim but he couldn't do much about that. He had married in a moment of weakness when she tricked him by getting pregnant. A costly commitment, but one that he could end now with impunity. He could restart his life and salvage his future now. All he had to do was carry through with his plan. Just the thought of a new lease on life energized him.

"Hon? I never thought it would be so hot out here. I'm thirsty." She smiled and shaded her eyes from the sun with her hand.

He smiled back. "I'll get you a drink." Perfect opportunity. He opened the cooler and pulled out the bottle with the pre-mixed drink. He poured it into a glass and added ice. Tasteless and odorless, she wouldn't notice a thing.

He walked slowly towards her and stilled his trembling hand. He bent over and kissed her on the cheek and set the glass beside her.

"Thanks, hon. I wish you got pictures of our new house. I can hardly wait to see it."

"I was so focused on closing the deal that I forgot. You'll see it soon enough." Melinda knew only what he had told her. He managed their finances and she had no clue that there was no house, no new job. In truth they were broke. He had blown through Melinda's inheritance, and his wealthy bankrolling parents didn't actually exist.

She had forced him to act sooner by getting pregnant again. Unplanned, just like the last time. That really pissed him off. Her carelessness forced him into action a few months earlier, which meant he hadn't really had enough time to set everything in motion yet.

As long as he wasn't sloppy he could improvise. The timing wasn't perfect, but the sooner he took care of things, the sooner his new life started. He felt a shiver of excitement as he imagined his newfound freedom.

He had planned everything down to the smallest detail. Even meticulous planners got busted, but he was smarter than most. On the true-crime shows, people inevitably missed some small detail, a fabric fiber or pet hair. Or a suspicious friend. He was smarter than most people, so he wouldn't slip up.

He also had a huge advantage most of those people didn't. Melinda had no siblings. Her parents had both died in a car accident five years ago and she had no other close relatives. She had few friends, and they hadn't known any of their high-rise neighbors.

His wife had already been forgotten by her co-workers. She had quit her minimum-wage retail job months earlier at his insistence. No one ever called or came around, either. Melinda was an unimportant person in an unimportant world. Her few friends and acquaintances would soon forget all about her after the tragic accident.

This time the husband would die too. A dead husband could hardly be a suspect.

He opened the fish box and checked his dinghy and pump for the umpteenth time. Lights, camera, action. Months of careful planning had rewarded him with a cloudless July day and the perfect tidal conditions to carry out his plan.

His fourteen-foot runabout was barely seaworthy, but adequate enough to sail in calm seas. The strait between Vancouver and Vancouver Island was reasonably calm in summer so he didn't expect any problems. He'd bought the boat just months ago and wished he didn't have to torch it. Any deviation from his careful plan though, and he'd be sunk, too. But if he stuck to the plan, he could buy dozens of better boats to replace it.

Georgia Strait bustled with summer traffic, a constant marine rush-hour of small pleasure craft and the large passenger ferries that ran between the mainland and the island as residents and tourists sailed back and forth. The summer wind was brisk but pleasant, providing a cooling effect from the heat that had enveloped the coast all week. Frank maintained a course slightly south, just far enough away from the commercial boats not to attract attention. They were already halfway across the strait to their destination, Victoria.

At least that was what he had told her. There was no new job or house in Victoria, but Melinda didn't know that. So far, so good. It was a fine day for the fresh start he had planned for months.

It was his mantra for his new life. Mantras and affirmations kept him moving towards his end goal. He had been living a lie for years now, but it was a necessary lie. He had been patient and now he could practically taste freedom. A few more hours and it was his.

He had sown the seeds for a successful future. Now it was harvest time.

A perfect July day.

The first day of the rest of his life.

It was cliché, but true. And he could hardly wait to start his next adventure. He patted the pocket of his cargo shorts, feeling the reassuring bulk of his new identification. Passport, driver's license, and high limit credit cards ready to go. Counterfeit, of course. He had already tested them a few days ago. They were all he needed to establish his new life.

Frank and Melinda had moved out of their rented Vancouver apartment and placed their furniture in storage, since their temporary new home in Victoria came fully furnished. They had sublet from a teacher who was away on a year-long sabbatical in India. It was the same teacher whose position Frank would assume for one year. He was due to start in September. At least that's what Melinda thought. It was all one big giant fabulous lie that she had bought into, hook, line and sinker. At long last his plan was underway.

The truth was something much different. There was no relocation, at least not for Melinda. That was the beauty of a work move. He pretended that the administrative people at the school had taken care of all the details, and that there wasn't enough time to consult Melinda. She could immerse herself in the details when she arrived in Victoria, he told her. Too bad for her that she never would.

But first they would enjoy one last day on the boat.

It had been exhausting, but so far everything had worked out on schedule. The neighbors, who they really didn't know—he had made sure of that—only discovered they were leaving yesterday, when he loaded the truck with their belongings destined for the storage locker. Four-year-old Emily was too young to attend school, and hadn't attended daycare since Melinda quit her job. No one in their tiny circle of acquaintances would notice them missing on Monday morning.

Melinda only knew what he told her, and he had been purposely short on details. She believed anything he said, no matter how outrageous. She was stupid in a bovine, trusting sort of way.

Or maybe not so stupid. She had tricked him with the pregnancy, knowing he had never wanted children, would never want them. She duped him, but he had some tricks of his own.

Melinda had weighed him down. She held him back from achieving his true potential and it was time to change things. Except the change didn't include a new city or teaching job. It didn't come with a new school and certainly no new fully furnished house to move into. The whole thing was a lie, a necessary one. It had taken a lot of work to get to this point, especially since he'd had to put the plan in place months earlier than he wanted. All because of Melinda.

Never look back.

His plan was working exactly as expected. He had the power to change his life now. Right now, like the seminar said. He had what it took to be successful. It was all up to him.

Now he just had to complete his plan.

Emily slept below deck, blissfully unaware of the sudden detour her life was about to take.

He hesitated. Maybe he could get divorced instead.

No. Too many loose ends. Child support would keep him tied to that cow for almost twenty years. That complicated things. He hated complications, and he hated being responsible for other people.

Never settle for less than you know you deserve.

He was glad he'd listened to his motivational recording this morning. Fresh in his mind, it helped reaffirm his convictions and gave him the strength to undertake the next step.

They had neared their destination hours ago but had circled back when he was overcome with a case of last-minute jitters. He was fine now, and Melinda was oblivious, as usual. He cut the engine and waited for Melinda to notice.

"Hon? Why are we stopped?" She slurped the last of her drink and placed the glass down beside her.

"I don't know. The engine stalled." He fiddled with the motor as he studied his wife. She was well on her way to unconsciousness.

Melinda yawned. "I'm falling asleep, must be the sun."

Her speech was slurred. The medication had kicked in.

Less than five minutes later she was comatose, her mumbled speech replaced by snores. Her right arm dropped off the lounge chair and landed with a thud on the deck. She didn't awaken.

Another ten minutes. Frank debated tying her wrists together, but that would be obvious foul play when her body turned up. What an interesting turn of words, foul play. A term with such gravity, yet it was called play. Or maybe it meant you played someone, as in trickery.

He got that feeling in the pit of his stomach again. What if something went horribly wrong and she awakened? Bound wrists prevented her from saving herself. Were there predators that might consume her flesh? He hadn't even thought about that.

In the end he decided to leave her wrists unbound. In the unlikely event her body was recovered, the ties would leave bruises. Those marks would not only be evidence of murder, but also provide information on the time of death. He dropped the rope onto the deck.

She was dead weight. He had given her a triple dose, so there was no way she would regain consciousness. He lifted her arm and dropped it to test his hypothesis.

No response.

Her arm was limp in his hand, dead weight.

He released it and it dropped to the ground.

He stepped back and studied her. He had positioned her lounge chair close to the edge, which made it easier to get her off the boat. He remembered his engineering theory from college and had rigged a crude sort of pulley system that he now attached to the chair.

His heart thumped in his chest, both from fear of discovery and the exhilaration of finally doing it. He didn't even feel an ounce of guilt.

He pulled the tarp out of the storage box and unfolded it. It was probably an unnecessary step since he was torching the boat, but you couldn't be too careful. He also hated the mess afterwards, and didn't want to make more work for himself.

Perspiration broke out on his brow as he dragged the deck chair as close to the edge as possible. He paused and wiped his brow, then unfurled the tarp and threw it over the top. He tucked the edges around the chair and then heaved it over the side.

No blood, DNA or other evidence. No mess.

Just a small, self-contained scene he could control, without worry of evidence showing up with Luminol or other forensic tools.

An extra precaution, maybe, since the boat would be burned. But you could never be too careful.

He took a deep breath and watched the lump sink into the ocean. He brushed his hands on his shorts just as the tarp floated to the top several feet away.

Damn. He hadn't thought of that.

He grabbed an oar and extended his arm as far as possible, but the tarp lay just out of reach.

He gasped as an arm protruded from the tarp. She hadn't sunk at all. She was still wrapped in the damn tarp.

"Daddy?"

Frank jumped, startled. He turned to face his daughter. "Emily? I thought you were sleeping."

"Where's Mommy?" She wore the overpriced pink and yellow flowered dress Melinda had picked out just for the occasion of moving to a new home. Just like Melinda to spend a small fortune on something frivolous.

"She's downstairs, honey." He had also slipped a sedative into Emily's juice when they left Vancouver. It should have knocked her out for hours. Instead, Emily was merely disheveled. Her hair was tangled. One tiny pink sandal was missing and the other was unbuckled.

Frank broke out in a sweat. What the hell had happened? Emily's dose had been half that of Melinda's, yet she weighed less than a third. What if Melinda's didn't take? What if the shock of the water woke her and she was somehow rescued?

"No she's not. Daddy, my head hurts." She rubbed her eyes and frowned. "Where's Mommy?"

He glanced at the tarp, where Melinda's leg was partially exposed as the buoyant tarp separated from her body. He had to fix that fast.

"She's having a nap, honey. Now go back to sleep." What if Melinda was discovered and rescued somehow? The strait had a lot of marine traffic on a summer day, so it was quite possible. Why hadn't he thought to weigh her down with cement like the mobsters did?

Whatever. He had always prided himself on thinking on his feet, and now was no different. He would adapt and move on.

"Why did you throw the chair overboard? Will that hurt the fishes?"

He felt a catch in his throat. How much had she seen? "Come here and give Daddy a kiss." He kneeled and held open his arms.

She shuffled forward with her half-sandaled feet and fell drowsily into his arms.

He caught her with one arm and clamped his other hand over her nostrils and mouth.

Emily tried to scream. She struggled against him, and her tiny arms flailed as she tried to breathe.

How long, he wondered.

Like a just caught fish struggling for its last breath.

He caught movement from the corner of his eye as the blue tarp unfurled in the waves. It was like a giant target as it floated on the water. Melinda's body had finally separated from the tarp and slowly sank below the surface. He watched as he held Emily and waited.

She stopped struggling in less than a minute and went limp. Careful not to uncover her mouth and nose, he loosened his grip on her body and checked her neck for a pulse. Nothing. He waited another minute to ensure she was dead, then tipped her overboard.

Just in time. He spotted the sailboat as it approached from the south. At the same time he noticed the wind had picked up. He looked down at the water where Emily had gone in. He expected to see ripples.

Except she hadn't sunk. She floated, face down in the water. Her pink rubber sandal still loosely attached to her foot. But all dead bodies were supposed to sink, at least that's what his research had indicated. What the hell?

That stupid dress again. The fabric trapped the air.

The sailboat was closer now, within 100 feet. Close enough for them to see him clearly, and perhaps even see Emily's body in the water. With binoculars they might have even seen what he did. He panicked and grabbed an oar. He plunged it into Emily's back, pushing her down below the waterline. The air pockets in her flouncy dress dispersed and down she went.

Then her sandal popped off her foot and floated on the water. He almost retrieved the shoe with the oar before he realized that would release Emily's body to the surface.

His heart pounded as the sailboat veered closer.

He swore under his breath. He had overlooked the most important thing. It hadn't occurred to him that the bodies might not sink immediately.

The sailboat straightened course and glided through the water less than fifty feet away. Only one man was visible on deck. He was busy adjusting the sails. "Thank God," he said aloud as he held his oar against Emily's body in the water. He raised his free arm and waved.

It was Melinda's fault for tricking him and getting pregnant. He wanted to enjoy life, something that was impossible with a baby, a stay-at-home wife and all the bills that were sure to follow. He was sick and tired of being manipulated and living with all the compromises he'd had to make. He only had one life to live and he wasn't about to waste it.

He pulled out his cell phone, wallet and keys and tossed them overboard. In the unlikely event they were found, it would appear that he went overboard with Melinda and Emily. His body would never be found, but he wasn't too worried about that. Many bodies went unrecovered in these waters. As long as nothing traced him to the torched the boat in the harbor, he should be fine.

It added a little bit of mystery and intrigue. He liked that. Might as well have a bit of fun outwitting them.

He glanced at his hand and noticed his wedding ring. He pulled it off his finger and studied it in the palm of his hand. It was symbolic, he thought as he tossed it overboard. Out with the old, in with the new.

A new life. A rich one. And it started right now.

Chapter 2

Katerina Carter's downtown office window framed a spectacular view of the Vancouver harbor. Great for daydreaming, not so great for getting work done. She checked her watch and realized two things: she had been staring out the window for a good twenty minutes, and her boyfriend, Jace Burton, was late.

Jace was always on time, but he should have arrived for their weekend getaway by now. They hadn't much time before their charter flight departed for De Courcy Island, a small, sparsely populated island in the Juan de Fuca Strait near Vancouver Island.

Jace's latest project for The Sentinel was historical lore based on a 1920s cult. According to Jace, the cult had plenty of scandal, sex, and even rumors of hidden treasure. The man behind it all went by the name Brother Twelve, or rather, Brother XII, as he insisted it be written. Apparently the Egyptian gods he communicated with had a thing for Roman numerals.

The trip was technically a working weekend for Jace. His Brother XII assignment was part of a historical series he wrote. Jace freelanced, so a long-term series like this was good. It provided both steady work and perks, like free trips all over North America, depending on the story.

This assignment was nearby, but it might as well have been thousands of miles away. De Courcy Island was located in the southern part of the Gulf Islands chain, nestled between Vancouver Island and Gabriola Island. The island was less than thirty miles offshore, yet accessible only by private boat or charter seaplane.

De Courcy was something of a ghost island. Like a ghost town, it was long past its heyday with only a few dozen residents. Less than a hundred years ago, De Courcy had been home to Brother XII's mysterious cult, the Aquarian Foundation. Soon after it started, the founder relocated the organization from Cedar-by-the-Sea on Vancouver Island to the more isolated De Courcy and Valdes Islands to escape public scrutiny and criticism.

Cults intrigued Kat. She was always fascinated at how charismatic leaders duped otherwise smart and savvy people. Brother XII was a perfect example. His real name was Edward Arthur Wilson. He claimed to have been born in India to a princess, though evidence suggested he was actually from a lower-middle-class background in Birmingham, England.

Brother XII based his cult upon the teachings of the Theosophical Society and attracted sizeable donations from thousands of wealthy individuals, including millionaire tycoons. They feared a financial Armageddon as the global financial markets collapsed.

He claimed that his New Age occultism would save them, and that they would be safe in the Aquarian Foundation's self-sufficient island settlements. Instead, the Aquarian Foundation went down in flames. Brother XII disappeared never to be seen again, leaving his followers in financial ruin.

Today the Aquarian Foundation was mostly forgotten, but in its heyday it had been a massive worldwide scandal. Funny how history repeated the same drama, with just minor changes to the cast and setting. People believed what they wanted to believe, even with overwhelming evidence to the contrary. Kat saw that every day as a forensic accountant and fraud investigator.

Carter & Associates, her forensic accounting and fraud investigation business, was busy and profitable, and she had worked extra hours to catch up before her long weekend trip. She was in a festive mood, ready for a few days of sun, sand and relaxation.

She had counted the days all week, anxious for a first-hand look at whatever remained of the settlement. She also planned to beachcomb while Jace researched Brother XII and the cult.

She checked her watch and felt a pang of anxiety. Jace was now a half-hour late, and they were in danger of missing their charter flight. She scanned the harbor and wondered which of the half-dozen floatplanes in the harbor was theirs.

"He's finally here, Kat." Uncle Harry slid into her office, surprisingly spry for his seventy-plus years. "That guy needs a new watch."

"Uncle Harry, slow down or you'll break a hip." Technically her uncle wasn't on Carter & Associates' payroll, yet he spent almost as much time at her office as she did. He had morphed into a permanent volunteer—and fixture—around the office. With no assigned duties, he had no real reason to be here. He was good company, though.

"Geez, Kat. I'm in great shape. Give me some credit." Harry spun sideways before he crashed against the wall. "Ouch."

"You okay?"

"Sure." He winced. "Yoga's gonna hurt tomorrow."

"You could take a day off." Uncle Harry's yoga was apparently an extreme sport, evidenced by his ever-present bruises. What possessed a septuagenarian man to sign up for yoga in the first place? Female septuagenarians, no doubt.

"I suppose. But then my flexibility would just go to pot. Oh, and Gia's here too."

"But we're already late." Kat and Gia Camiletti had been close friends since the third grade. She had hadn't seen or heard from Gia for weeks and wanted to catch up with her, but now wasn't the time.

"She's with some hot young guy." Harry bent over to touch his toes. He reached mid-calf before he grunted and returned upright.

A flowery perfume scent wafted into Kat's office, followed seconds later by Gia in a bright fuchsia-flowered sleeveless dress with matching four-inch heels. All five-foot-two of her curvaceous jiggle tugged at her dress seams. She was twenty pounds more than her dress could handle. "Kat! Meet my new boyfriend, Raphael."

Raphael was drop-dead gorgeous, on par with the best-looking movie or reality TV stars. The guy on Gia's arm didn't even seem real. His Mediterranean tan contrasted against his tailored white linen shirt. The partially unbuttoned shirt imparted a casual look and also exposed a muscular chest. He wore cotton pants and expensive-looking loafers.

"A pleasure to meet you." Raphael smiled and kissed Kat's hand with an exaggerated flourish. His veneers flashed so white they were almost ultraviolet. His shirt clung to his skin from the heat outside, accentuating broad shoulders and a lean torso. He was more perfect than an airbrushed magazine model, if that was possible.

Kat was immediately suspicious. Guys like Raphael rarely gravitated towards plump hair stylists like Gia. While he was naturally good-looking, it was obvious he had spent money on his appearance too. Most men cared little for expensive clothing or dental work. Maybe he was vain, or maybe he saw it as an investment of sorts.

She was also surprised to see Gia with Raphael since she had sworn off men after her high school sweetheart had left her at the altar two years ago. The groom never showed—or even called—leaving Gia humiliated and vowing revenge.

"Kat?" Gia pulled her beau closer. "Don't just stare. Say hi."

Kat flushed, embarrassed as she already imagined Raphael's demise at the hands of Gia. At least she hoped that would happen. This guy gave her the creeps. She mumbled a hello.

Raphael held her hand a moment longer than necessary and stared seductively into her eyes. He was as cool as rain and she instinctively distrusted him.

It was obvious what attracted Gia. The guy looked like he hit the gym for a couple of hours a day. Gia, on the other hand, wouldn't be caught dead in a gym. Despite his model good looks he just didn't seem like the kind of guy that would make Gia happy. Someone like Raphael would only make Gia feel more insecure about herself. He was tall, tanned, and totally out of Gia's league. His polished look was straight from the pages of a men's magazine.

Raphael also seemed to be the polar opposite of Gia's quirky and offbeat style. While Gia's infectious enthusiasm was fun, men like Raphael tended to go more for looks than personality. It was wrong to make snap judgments about the guy, but her instincts were usually right on the money.

Raphael bent over and planted a kiss on Gia's forehead while still clasping Kat's hand. "Bellissima, you didn't mention your gorgeous friend." He turned to Kat and looked her up and down before casting a dismissive glance at her office.

"She's smart, too." Gia winked at Kat. "Kat's a forensic accountant. She investigates fraud."

Raphael dropped Kat's hand like she was radioactive. From gorgeous to toxic in mere seconds. "Raphael buys and sells businesses." Gia beamed at him. "He just arrived from Italy and closed a multi-million dollar deal for the North American line of his revolutionary hair products. We're moving in together."

"Interesting." It was all Kat could say without betraying her suspicions. Gia was her childhood friend and told Kat everything. She knew for a fact that Gia had no man in her life just a couple of weeks ago, yet they were making plans to move in together. It was like Raphael had just materialized out of thin air. Everything was moving way too fast.

Gia's brows furrowed as she studied Kat. "That's all you can say? I thought you'd be fascinated. Business deals are right up your alley."

"I'd love to hear the details, but we're late for our trip." She should be happy for Gia, but instead she was annoyed. Not at her friend, but towards Raphael. Within minutes of meeting him, she felt insecure and inadequate in her shabby little office. She resented that, since she was proud of the business she had built from nothing. But compared to Raphael, it looked like she hadn't achieved very much at all.

What could possibly be revolutionary in hair products? She was a cynic when it came to beauty products. Shampoo was just glorified soap, repackaged and marketed to gullible consumers—and hair stylists. She'd stick with her drugstore shampoo instead of overpriced salon products, though she'd never admit that to Gia.

Gia, a hair stylist, thought differently. Every new shampoo or styling aid was like man's discovery of fire or something. She chided Kat at every haircut for using cheap hair products. Kat promised to switch if Gia somehow proved her salon products were better. Of course Gia couldn't, because there was no scientific proof or formula difference in the products.

"Kat?" Jace stood behind the couple, a duffle bag slung over one shoulder.

Raphael immediately turned and introduced himself. The two men shook hands as Gia smiled at Kat.

He turned to Raphael and introduced himself.

Rescued at last. She motioned to Jace and tapped her watch. "We're late, Jace. We'll miss the flight if we don't leave now."

"One sec. Just got a text from the airline." Jace frowned as he studied his phone screen. Even with his head bowed he almost reached the top of the door frame. He was several inches taller than Raphael, but lanky and wiry in contrast to Raphael's muscular physique.

Harry pushed past Jace into the room. He held out a hand to Raphael. "I'm Harry Denton, Kat's associate." In reality Carter & Associates was associate-less, but Harry liked the bustle of the office and worked part-time. He wasn't very tech-savvy so there wasn't much for him to do other than reception and the odd bit of filing. Clients loved him though, and it was nice to have company at the office. It was a win-win situation for both of them.

Raphael shook his hand. "What exactly does an-uh, associate do around here?"

"I help Kat with the fraud investigations." Harry pointed at Kat. "She's uncovered some doozies. In the billions, even, like the Liberty blood diamond case."

"Really?" Raphael stiffened and scanned her office in distaste. "I'd never guess that from the looks of this place."

Kat flushed. "I usually meet my clients at their office, so there's no need for appearances." She immediately regretted her answer. She had practically insulted herself. Now she just sounded defensive.

"I would probably do the same." Raphael turned away.

Was he implying her office wasn't worthy of guests? Substance trumped appearances in Kat's books any day. She disliked Raphael already. What gave him the right to march in here and criticize her office?

"I've got some renovations planned. This place just needs a little elbow grease," Harry wiped his forehead. "I've got to redo the hardwood floors, add a fresh coat of paint and wainscoting.

There's just never enough time in the day. I always get sidetracked."

Raphael laughed. "You've got your work cut out for you."

Whatever. She liked her early twentieth-century Gastown office just the way it was. Shabby-chic, with its exposed wood and large windows that framed the harbor view. Unfashionable also meant cheap rent and low overhead. Just ignore him, she reminded herself.

She dropped her laptop in her bag and stood, ready to go. She counted the seconds until she could leave Gia's rude boyfriend behind.

Jace frowned as he looked up from his cell phone. "I hate to tell you this, but our flight's cancelled. Mechanical problems, with no other flights till Tuesday."

"That's terrible." Kat sighed. An August weekend away with Jace on a chartered plane to a sparsely populated island, all expenses paid? Of course it had been too good to be true. "Maybe next weekend?"

Jace shrugged. "I can't wait that long. My deadline is next Friday. I'll need to find another way to get there."

"Why don't I take you to De Courcy Island?" Raphael motioned to the harbor view. "On my yacht."

"A blessing in disguise!" Gia clapped her hands together. "Now we can hang out together."

Gia's boyfriend has a yacht? This was quickly becoming unbelievable.

"Uh, no. I can't impose on you like that." Jace dropped his duffel bag on Kat's office chair. "You two must have other plans."

Yes, please have other plans. Kat sized people up pretty quickly and was certain Raphael was up to no good. What did Gia see in him?

Silly question. Raphael was not only handsome but apparently rich as well.

"Not really, and it's no trouble at all," Raphael said. "I've always wanted to explore the islands. This is the perfect opportunity."

Gia's bracelets jingled as she jumped up and down on her four-inch heels. "It'll be so much fun! We'll have time to visit, and Jace can write his story. We can explore the island and relax onboard afterwards!"

Jace shifted his weight from one foot to another. "If you're absolutely sure, that would be great. I really do have a deadline to meet and the only other way there is by boat. I can chip in some money for fuel…"

"Maybe there's another airline…" Kat's mind raced. Yacht fuel was probably thousands of dollars. Jace didn't realize what he was agreeing to.

"Don't be ridiculous." Raphael laughed. "I was headed over that way anyways. What's your story about?"

"A 1920s cult, complete with a sex scandal and hidden treasure," Jace said. "A guy named Brother XII founded the Aquarian Foundation in 1927. He claimed it was a spiritual community waiting for the Age of Aquarius. But the price of admission was high. He sought out only wealthy members. Since he took everybody's money, it was either a cult, scam or both."

"Scam," said Kat. "A cult is almost always a scam. Especially when the first order of business is to convince the followers to turn over all their money."

Raphael scoffed. "You're a glass half-empty type, I see."

Kat frowned.

Gia mouthed sorry to Kat and tugged on Raphael's arm. "I love treasure-hunting!"

"I didn't mean that the way it sounded," Raphael said. "In my experience though, the bean counters are always the naysayers. They always say no when everyone else says yes."

Jace laughed. "Realists, for sure, but there's a benefit. Kat's better than anyone at sniffing criminals out. She gets the money back, too."

They talked about her like she wasn't even there. She opened her mouth to respond but stopped herself. Jace hadn't interpreted Raphael's comment as rude, so maybe she was overreacting. It sure felt like an insult though. But she didn't want to start an argument, so she just gritted her teeth and smiled.

"Brother XII sounds like an intriguing guy," Raphael said.

"Charismatic at least," Jace said. "His real name was Edward Arthur Wilson. He claimed to be the reincarnation of the Egyptian god Osiris, and his Aquarian Foundation was based on the premise of an impending doomsday. He claimed the end was near, and only a few chosen believers would have their souls saved."

"People fell for that?" Raphael arched his brows. "Not too smart."

"Surprisingly, most were very smart, educated people," Jace said. "One of the Aquarian Foundation's board members was a prominent international newspaper publisher. He got a lot of press from his publications and others too. That gave Brother XII a worldwide audience. Soon he had thousands of affluent and influential followers, even presidential candidates.

"They contributed millions to Wilson and his Aquarian Foundation and he used the funds to establish a self-contained society and settlement with Wilson at the helm. Hundreds of people worldwide moved here to join him, most handing over all their worldly possessions."

"They had to be crazy to give their money to him," Gia said. "Who would risk losing it like that?"

"Surprising what people will do," Raphael stroked his chin. "They'll pay huge sums of money to get what they want. It's not always about money and wealth. Sometimes they just want to be part of something bigger than themselves."

Jace nodded. "Hindsight is 20/20. Raphael's right. Most of them were already wealthy. What they really wanted was to be accepted and belong to something. Brother XII fulfilled that need. In the mid-1920s he published a series in England in The Occult Review. He claimed psychic abilities and that Armageddon was imminent. It was easy to convince his initial followers to join him in 1927. Lucky for Brother XII, they were all wealthy, and they each surrendered all of their assets to him and the Aquarian Foundation."

"Why would anyone do that?" Harry asked. "That's insane."

"I think so too," Jace said. "But they were caught up with the idea that they were about to enter the new Age of Aquarius. They expected a day of reckoning and figured this put them on the right side of the fence when Armageddon finally did hit.

Plus, Brother XII made them feel special by inviting only twelve people at first."

Raphael nodded appreciatively. "Invitation only. Nice concept."

"I wouldn't be fooled by that," Harry said.

"You'd be surprised," Jace said. "There was a lot of hype in the press. People saw it as a once-in-a-lifetime opportunity. Besides, what good was their money if the world was about to end?"

"I can see that," Gia added. "All the newspapers carried his claims, so it stood to reason that people got swept up in the hysteria."

"Exactly," Jace agreed. "And Brother XII's wealthy converts were suspicious of the naysayers' motives, so they dismissed any accusations against Brother XII."

"Smart man, even if he was a crook." Raphael clapped his hands. "Well? What are we waiting for? Let's go to De Courcy Island. We can walk to the ship. I'm docked down in the marina."

"Ooh, a real adventure!" Gia exclaimed. "I can't wait."

"Me too! Let me get my things." Uncle Harry ran from Kat's office before she could protest. Her romantic getaway with Jace had somehow morphed into a party. But Jace needed the story, so who was she to argue?

Chapter 3

Raphael's yacht, *The Financier*, turned out to be more than a hundred-and-fifty feet, the largest in the marina by far. Its pristine white hull gleamed in the afternoon sun as they headed down the gangway, bags in tow.

Kat had worked for many millionaires and a few billionaires in her prior job as an international finance consultant. She had seen her share of tycoon toys and had even attended parties on some of them. She knew little about yachts, but *The Financier* was larger and more lavishly appointed than any she had been on. Raphael's yacht dwarfed all the other boats in the marina in both size and splendor.

Kat felt envious stares upon them as they trudged down the dock behind Raphael and Gia. The attention gave her a strange sense of importance, like she was a celebrity or something.

The afternoon sun beat down on them as they boarded *The Financier*. They immediately headed below deck to a spacious air-conditioned galley and a hallway that led to the rear, or aft, of the ship. The luxurious interior was finished in expensive-looking teak built-in furniture and lighting. Raphael motioned towards a cabin on the right. Jace had cancelled their accommodations as Raphael had insisted that they stay aboard the yacht.

"That one's for you two, and Harry's is next-door," Raphael said.

Kat followed Jace inside their cabin. It was more spacious than she expected, at least double the size of the stateroom on their Caribbean cruise last year. "Wow."

She dropped her bag on the bed and ducked back out into the passageway. She peeked in Harry's suite next door. It was smaller but no less luxurious.

"I could sure get used to this." Harry peered out the large porthole. "Maybe I'll become a merchant seaman, get a job on board."

Kat laughed. "You're over seventy, Uncle Harry. Too late to look for a new job, and you've already got a pension. Besides, I'll bet the crew works very hard to keep everything running."

Kat exited her uncle's stateroom and peered down the hall. Beyond Harry's stateroom were the crew's quarters. According to Raphael, the ship was equipped with all the latest technology and navigation. She had yet to see the crew, but they were probably busy preparing for departure.

She returned to her stateroom, where Jace unpacked his duffel into the built-in bureau.

"This yacht must be worth more than our house." She sat on the bed and ran her hand over the Egyptian cotton duvet cover. She was happy for Gia but felt that her love affair with Raphael was a little too good to be true. Everything about him was just too perfect.

"More than several houses, I'm sure." Jace laughed. "I'm glad Raphael didn't take me up on my offer to pay for gas. When he said 'yacht', I thought he was exaggerating."

"Apparently not. Don't you find that Gia and Raphael make an odd couple?" Raphael's tailored clothes, perfect physique and, apparently, billionaire status bordered on unbelievable. Not that Gia wasn't a catch for any guy. Just that guys didn't normally see it that way.

Gia was fun, attractive, and successful, but she wasn't exactly a swimsuit model. Guys like Raphael typically went for image and looks. The women that decorated their arms were often an extension of that.

"Kind of." Jace shrugged. "They seem to like each other a lot, though. Good for Gia."

Kat intended to check out Raphael to see if he was who he claimed to be. She'd expose him soon enough.

"I suppose." She only had a few stolen moments with Jace before they headed back upstairs, and she wanted to gauge his impression of Raphael. "Are you sure about this, Jace? I feel weird imposing on Raphael. We barely know him."

"You heard him," Jace said. "He said he always wanted to visit the islands. If I had a boat like this, I'd be looking for excuses to go places. I've got to find some way to repay him, though. Maybe I can do some business writing for him or something."

"I guess." Kat still felt uneasy. Raphael probably had an ulterior motive; she just didn't know what it was yet. He gave her the creeps but she had nothing tangible to base her feelings on. But her gut told her there was something wrong about him.

"Gia told me he lives aboard," Jace said. "Can you imagine a life like that? This ship must be worth millions."

"It must be hard to travel and manage business from half a world away," Kat said. "I'll bet it costs a fortune to operate this thing."

Jace sat beside her on the bed. "He has a fortune. I'm sure he doesn't worry about it."

"Must come from a very wealthy family," Kat said. "He's far too young to have earned all this money himself." Where did Raphael find the time to sail from Italy in the midst of his new business launch? Most tycoons had no time for impromptu yacht trips.

"Maybe he'll let us in on his secret," Jace said. "Wouldn't it be wonderful to live like this?"

"It's very luxurious," Kat agreed. Their stateroom was sumptuously appointed right down to luxurious Egyptian cotton and damask bedding and original seascape oil paintings. "Why don't you write a story about how he achieved his success? We'll be spending a lot of time with him. You can get two assignments instead of just your Brother XII assignment."

"That's a great idea. He's a fascinating guy. A lot of people would be interested in how he made his fortune."

"I'm sure they would." She was one of them, since she doubted Raphael's riches came honestly. Quick riches often meant shortcuts, and her instincts told her he had taken some. How many people had he burned in his climb to the top? Jace's story might provide some answers. "You can find out his secrets."

Jace winked. "I intend to."

"I'm worried about Gia." On the one hand, she was glad for Gia. She deserved happiness. But Gia's whirlwind romance with Raphael made Kat uneasy. She was infatuated to the extent that she wasn't seeing things—and Raphael—clearly. "Maybe you could find out more about his background, see if he checks out."

"I'm not going to interrogate him, if that's what you mean." Jace shook his head. "Gia can take care of herself just fine. If she's not worried, why are you?"

Gia had a knack for business, having built her salon from scratch without any help. But she was very naïve about men and Kat doubted she applied the same critical eye when it came to romance. "I just hope he doesn't break her heart."

"You're making snap judgments about the guy." Jace wrapped an arm around her waist. "You have to admit that it's pretty generous of him to take us all to De Courcy Island."

"I guess, but everything's so sudden. Gia just met him a couple of weeks ago and they're already serious about each other." She needed to speak with Gia privately, and soon.

Her uneasiness about Raphael grew, though she couldn't put her finger on why. It was as if he were falling in love on a deadline. Love rarely stuck to a schedule, let alone an aggressive one. If Raphael had a hidden agenda, she needed to find out why. A little surreptitious digging wouldn't hurt as long as she did it secretly.

"I still can't believe Gia's dating a guy with a yacht this size. He must be worth at least a hundred mil."

"Jace, Gia's doing pretty well herself. She's opened two profitable salons in five years." Gia's hard work and financial acumen had paid off. Underneath Gia's bubbly exterior was a shrewd businesswoman with a talent for entrepreneurship. "Her Curl Up n' Dye franchise is very successful already. She doesn't need Raphael to be successful."

Kat was proud of her friend's single-handed success. Kat had watched Gia's business grow and had helped her with financial advice since she started her salon business ten years ago.

"She might not need him, but it's nice to share your hopes and dreams with someone." Jace pulled her close and kissed her. "It makes all the hard work worthwhile."

Kat sighed as she stood. "Gia deserves happiness, but something doesn't add up for me. I don't know exactly what it is yet, but I'm a little worried."

"Just be glad for her, Kat. Don't mess things up by interrogating him or being suspicious. " Jace shook his head and walked towards the door. "Not everyone's a criminal."

Maybe not, but Raphael certainly had the outward appearance of the many scoundrels she had encountered as a fraud investigator.

"I know. I just couldn't live with myself if my suspicions were true and I did nothing." Spending so much time around white-collar criminals gave her a cynical outlook. "Of course I'm happy for her. I just don't want to see her get hurt."

"You're just envious. We don't have that kind of money and probably never will." Jace sighed. "I'll admit I'm a bit envious too. But let's mind our own business, okay?"

Jace couldn't be more different than Raphael. He wasn't hell bent on accumulating or displaying wealth or status. She and Jace weren't exactly rich, but they had everything they needed and were doing just fine. But maybe he was right. She was envious. If his displays of wealth and affection were true, that is. She suspected trouble, though.

Jace held the door open as they exited their stateroom. "Look at it this way, Raphael is way more successful than Gia. If anyone should worry, it's him, not her."

The engines rumbled to life and vibrated beneath her feet as she ascended the stairs to the upper deck. While Raphael's offer to ferry them to De Courcy Island was generous, it was also guaranteed to impress them. Was it all part of Raphael's plan? Something didn't add up, and she intended to find out why.

Chapter 4

Kat and Jace emerged on deck to blinding sunlight. The rays reflected off the yacht's gleaming white fiberglass and chrome. Raphael's yacht was immaculate, outfitted with the latest equipment. They headed towards the stern, where they had agreed to regroup at the outdoor bar.

Kat traced her hand along the rail and recoiled as the metal scorched her skin. She was caught momentarily off balance as the ship got underway. The berth seemed to move as the vessel backed out of its spot in the marina.

She decided to dig into Raphael's background a bit more. Her fears would be allayed if he checked out, and Gia would never know. Assuming he was legit. If he wasn't, the more she knew, the better she could warn Gia that her billionaire boyfriend was in reality a scam artist. Kat's intuition told her he was simply too good to be true.

Gia and Raphael stood arm in arm at the stern. They leaned against the railing with the harbor as a backdrop. They were such an unlikely couple. Fit Raphael, with his Mediterranean looks and tailored clothing contrasted sharply with plump Gia, who could stand to lose a few pounds. Her too-tight dress was a cheap designer knock-off, meant for someone younger and skinnier. How long before Raphael traded her in for a supermodel? Her bubbly personality wouldn't hold his attention for long.

Gia smiled. "I wondered where you two were. Let's enjoy the view while we leave the harbor."

Apparently they were the main attraction, judging by the dozen or so people who stopped in their tracks and stared as *The Financier* navigated the marina. The attention gave her a heady feeling. This must be what celebrities experienced when they were recognized. The trappings of wealth always attracted admiring stares.

Kat had hoped to catch Gia alone. She assumed Raphael would be busy as the ship departed, but that wasn't the case. Raphael's crew had everything well in hand and his help wasn't necessary.

Uncle Harry materialized at her side and patted her arm. "Isn't this grand? Forget about working aboard. I'll stowaway instead. Just keep mum when I don't get off the boat, okay?"

"Sure." She smiled. While she had simpler tastes, cruising certainly wasn't hard to get used to.

They exited the marina and set a westerly course out of the harbor towards the open ocean. The scenery slipped by as the boat gathered speed. The North Shore Mountains loomed larger and were now situated on their right—or was that starboard?—instead of straight ahead.

Raphael and Jace discussed yachting as Uncle Harry joined them a few feet away at the stern. They watched the yacht's wake as they headed out into the harbor.

Gia waved Kat over to a small table where she sat alone. "I can't wait to tell you everything. Isn't he amazing?"

Kat glanced over at the men as she sat down. They stood several feet away, engrossed in talk about engine speed and other guy things. Finally she could talk to Gia alone and learn more about her new love interest.

She sat opposite Gia at the table. "What a perfect day to be out on the water."

Gia nodded. "Drink?" Gia held a martini glass filled with fluorescent pink liquid and pointed at the well-stocked bar a few feet away.

Kat shook her head. "I'll just have water." She took a sip from the water bottle she had brought for the trip.

Gia gulped her drink. "I never ever imagined dating a billionaire."

"Billionaire?" At least Gia had broached the subject of Raphael's background. Now she could ask questions without seeming intrusive. "He's that wealthy?"

Gia giggled. "He's rich, hot, and totally into me. Crazy, huh? I can't even remember my life before Raphael. I'm madly in love with him."

"How long have you known him?"

"Long enough to know we'll spend the rest of our lives together."

Finally an answer, just not the one Kat had hoped for. "Don't rush things, Gia. You've known him a week, two weeks?" Gia hadn't mentioned a new man when they met for dinner a couple of weeks ago.

Gia twirled her half empty glass in her hand. "I know everything I need to already. He's a fascinating guy."

"He's pretty young to have so much money. Is his family wealthy?"

Gia nodded as she set her empty glass on the table. "They are now, because of the product Raphael and his mom invented a couple of years ago. They did it all themselves. None of that dot-com technology stuff. They made a hair product, of all things! Isn't that a coincidence?"

"An amazing coincidence. Have you tried it?"

"Not yet. But he's making me a part of the company." Gia blew a kiss to Raphael. "Isn't that fantastic?"

"But what about your salon? How will you find time to work for him?"

"Not as an employee, silly. As an investor," Gia said. "My experience in the North American beauty industry is something they need and want."

Kat raised her brows.

"I can get them a foothold into that market here."

Gia's salon was a local success story, but that hardly qualified her as a North American business expert. "How will you market and sell the product?"

"Raphael has it all planned out. I'll be on the ground executing the business plan. He said I'm perfect since I really understand the business." She squeezed Kat's hand. "Isn't this great? I never dreamed that I'd meet the love of my life in the beauty supply business. We have this incredible product.

Bellissima is a hair straightener that's about to take the beauty world by storm."

"Like a Brazilian Blowout or something?" Kat had tried the semi-permanent straightening method on her hair once, but decided a little frizz was better than a whole lot of chemicals on her head.

"Sort of, but much better. A Brazilian Blowout is just temporary. Bellissima permanently straightens your hair. As in forever."

"Have you even seen it? How does it work?" If the product was so lucrative, why hadn't one of the big cosmetics and beauty products companies already developed it? They had armies of scientists, product developers, and million-dollar budgets. It struck her as odd that Raphael and his mother could cook up a better product.

Gia turned and shrugged. "Ask Raphael. All I know is that he's already made a fortune with Bellissima in Europe."

"What's the name of his company?" Kat intended to dig up everything possible on Raphael. Since Gia had thrown caution to the wind, she needed to look out for her friend.

"I don't know, some Italian name. Your paranoia about all this is absolutely ridiculous."

"You're Italian, yet you can't remember an Italian name?" If Raphael's company was so successful, why did he need Gia's money in the first place? Why hadn't he gone to the bank? Kat hesitated. Gia would be angry no matter what she said, so she might as well ask. "Did you check out his claims to make sure they're true?"

"You think he lied about it all? Why would he do that?" Gia's face flushed with anger. "Honestly, Kat. You're unbelievable."

"I'm not saying that. It's just good to verify things."

"Our relationship is based on trust. Why would I ask when there's proof right here." Gia waved her arm. "The guy has this yacht, for crying out loud. He's legit."

"How does he find the time to sail around on his yacht? Doesn't he have a business to run?"

"It's called delegation, Kat. That's what rich people do. Their minions do the work." Gia tossed back her hair in an exaggerated flourish. "Their minions and their capital. You should try it sometime."

Their conversation had completely derailed. On the one hand, Kat wished she had never asked about Raphael and his company. On the other hand, Gia was in far too deep. She had to argue whether she wanted to or not. "You never said where you met him."

"That's the best part. He just walked into my salon. He said it looked just like his mama's salon back home. Isn't that a coincidence?"

Kat believed more in cons than coincidences. "That's interesting."

"It's a lot more than interesting. My whole life has changed in less than a week."

"You're being dramatic. You're just infatuated with him."

Gia shook her head. "No, it's so much more than that. I've met my soul mate, Kat. He's the man I'll spend the rest of my life with."

Before Gia could say another word, Raphael appeared at her side. He wrapped his arm possessively around her shoulder. "Everything good, bellissima?"

"È perfetto." Gia beamed up at him.

He bent over and kissed her forehead. He turned and rejoined Jace and Harry. They motored through Burrard Inlet, headed towards the open ocean.

Gia beamed. "Not only is he the man of my dreams, he's even Italian!"

"He hasn't got an accent. He sounds just like one of us."

Gia shook her head slowly. "Of course he doesn't have an accent. He went to an international boarding school. He's also fluent in seven languages."

"Oh. Sounds like he's good at everything." More like a good actor, but why had he chosen Gia to practice on?

"Don't be jealous, Kat. Let's not go back to grade school again." Gia seemed pleased at Kat's reaction.

Raphael glanced at them momentarily before turning back to the other men.

"How much did you invest, Gia?"

Silence.

"Gia, have you thought about what you're doing? You just met this guy, and he asked for money?"

"I'm a grown woman, Kat. I can think for myself."

At that, Raphael paused whatever he was saying and all three men looked over. A few seconds later they returned to their conversation.

Kat lowered her voice. "I'm just concerned that you haven't thought this through, Gia."

Harry rose from the table and Kat overheard him tell Jace and Raphael he was headed to the bridge to check out the navigation. That gave her an idea for later. Raphael's crew might be less reluctant to talk about their boss, or at least the yacht's travels. She could at least verify his claims about sailing from Italy. A casual conversation ought not to raise suspicion.

"He didn't ask, Kat. I offered."

Kat raised her brows.

"Okay, I practically begged him to let me in on it." Gia tucked a stray lock of hair behind her ear. "He didn't want to, but I insisted. It's an investment in my future. Our future."

Kat felt sick to her stomach. A growing sense of dread told her that whatever Raphael was up to, it wasn't good. Gia was too infatuated to see it.

Raphael and Jace joined them and Kat's hopes of continued conversation with Gia faded. Raphael wore a blank expression, but Jace appeared irritated, probably a result of overhearing snippets of her conversation with Gia.

Raphael pulled his chair beside Gia's and rested his arm on the back of her chair. "Such a great day to be out on the water."

"This beats a charter flight any day. I can't tell you how much I appreciate this." Jace placed his beer on the table and leaned back in his chair. He turned to Raphael. "I'd also like to do a story on you, if you're interested."

Raphael laughed. "You sure about that? I'll just bore everyone."

"Definitely not. People are fascinated with success. You especially. You're not even forty and you're living the dream. Want to spill your secrets?"

Perfect, Kat thought. She'd just absorb whatever Raphael told Jace, then fact check later.

"No secret, just knowing what to invest in and following my gut," Raphael said. "Timing is everything."

"What's your gut telling you now?" He would be short on details, since there weren't any.

Raphael smiled. "I've got the most amazing opportunity right now. I'd share it with you guys, but it's too early."

Gia tugged on his arm. "Kat and Jace are my closest friends. They're like family. You can tell them. They won't tell a soul." She glanced at Kat as if to say I told you so.

"I don't know, Gia." Raphael turned to Kat and Jace. "I want to tell you, but I'm bound by a confidentiality agreement."

"They can keep a secret. Tell them, sweetie." Gia giggled. "I already spilled some of the beans to Kat. I want to let her in on it too, so she can make huge profits like I have."

"All right, what the hell," Raphael said. "I'll make an exception. My ass is on the line though. Breathe a word of this and I'll have to kill you and throw you overboard."

Jace laughed. "Promise we can keep a secret."

Raphael leaned over and kissed Gia on the forehead. "You tell them, sweetheart."

Gia pulled her chair closer and leaned in to the table. She spoke in a whisper. "Raphael's new hair product is simply amazing. It's a patented hair straightening product called Bellissima and it's the best invention since shampoo."

"Why are you whispering?" Jace asked. "Who could possibly overhear us out here?"

"You can't be too careful." Gia looked over her shoulder towards mid-ship. "Bellissima is revolutionary. It's like getting a permanent wave, only in reverse. You put it on curly hair and it straightens it. Forever."

Gia sounded like an infomercial as she repeated what she had already told Kat.

Gia placed her hand on her chest. "I'm the exclusive North American distributor. Every salon will have to buy from me. It will launch just after the Oscars. We've got a promotion deal with a few A-list stars, and we'll have salon certificates in the Oscar swag bags. Raphael's thought of everything!"

The Oscars weren't until February, and it was only August. Raphael could be long gone by then. Why had Gia invested without trying the product? She was, after all, a stylist. A hair product was within her area of expertise.

"What makes Raphael's product so special from the others?" Jace asked.

Gia suddenly tugged on a clump of Kat's hair.

"Ouch!" Kat's hands flew to the back of her head. Gia was angrier than she thought. "You just pulled my hair out!"

Gia released her grip and smoothed Kat's hair. "This frizz would be gone with just one application and a blow dry."

"What frizz?" Kat pushed Gia's hand away, annoyed. She had temporarily straightened her hair with a flat iron this morning and thought it looked pretty good. It wasn't even humid out, so how could her hair possibly be frizzy? Or maybe Gia was avenging her earlier comments about Raphael.

Jace and Raphael tuned out at the mention of her hair. The men rose from the table. Jace frowned at Kat, then turned and followed Raphael to the rail.

Gia sighed. "Don't be so defensive. You can't help the hair you were born with. You can change it, though. Bellissima transforms frizz and curls into sleek straight hair."

"You invested in a product you haven't even tried yet? What proof do you have that it really works?"

"Gee, Kat. Do you really think I'm that dumb?" She shook her head. "I'll see the product next week when I fly to Italy with Raphael. We can't use it now and risk it falling into the wrong hands before the North American patent is registered. It's just like the Coke™® formula. Knowing the secret recipe could put my life in danger. I could be kidnapped or something."

"You mean like corporate espionage? That's ridiculous." The product was already for sale in Europe, so there was no added risk. Something didn't add up.

"Go ahead and make fun of me, but Bellissima is a game-changer. The other products only work temporarily. Bellissima is forever."

"Isn't that a bad thing?" Kat asked.

Gia frowned. "How so?"

"No chance of repeat customers. A single application of Bellissima straightener translates to zero repeat business. No other products or straightening treatments ever again. You'd have to charge a fortune for it."

Gia dismissed her with a wave of her hand, but she had struck a chord. "Talk to Raphael. It worked in Europe so it will work here. Once it's in the Hollywood Oscar Awards swag bag and the stars use it, everyone will want it. We'll make a killing!"

"I'm surprised you invested your money without knowing more specifics, Gia." Kat shifted in her chair.

"I know enough, Kat. As a stylist I just know this product will be huge. And Raphael didn't even ask me if I wanted in. I had to convince him to take my money in the first place."

"Is that right?" Raphael, like all scammers, appeared to be well-versed in psychology.

"Yes, that's right." Gia sniffed. "Now I wish I never told you in the first place. Here I am offering you a chance to make a fortune too, but all you do is criticize. Do you have to fight me every step of the way?"

"I appreciate that, but you haven't told me anything about the product." Kat shifted in her chair. "I thought these straightening products were banned. Don't they contain formaldehyde or something dangerous?"

Gia shook her head. "That's what's so revolutionary about Bellissima. It's completely natural."

"If it's completely natural, how can it be patented?"

"Anything can be patented. Human genes, varieties of corn, you name it."

The lighthearted mood had evaporated. "I'd still want more details before putting money in. If it's completely natural, why has no one discovered it before now?"

"Raphael can give you all the details. You can number-crunch to your heart's content."

Kat seriously doubted Raphael would be so forthcoming. Her weekend away was quickly turning into a new case, albeit a very personal one.

Chapter 5

The Financier motored through Active Pass and headed north through the Juan de Fuca Strait. A stiff breeze cooled the ocean air, welcome relief from Vancouver's sweltering summer temperatures. Harry and Gia played cards below deck in the air-conditioned galley while Jace and Raphael sat on the deck and discussed yachting.

Kat sat alone a few feet away on a patio lounge chair. She was out of earshot but unable to concentrate, knowing that Gia was in trouble. She reread the same page in her mystery novel over and over, unable to absorb the story. She couldn't stop thinking about Gia and Raphael. Regardless of Gia's claims, her gut told her that her friend was close to making a terrible mistake.

With a few general questions she had angered both Jace and Gia, but they were questions that had to be asked. Someone had to, and she couldn't just sit back and watch her friend get taken advantage of. It was hard enough remaining civil to Raphael.

While she had no proof he was anyone other than who he claimed, she always trusted her instincts. The man was hiding something and she wouldn't rest until she uncovered his secret.

A change of scenery was exactly what she needed to formulate a strategy. She rose and walked slowly around the deck to stretch her legs. There were ways to check Raphael out without angering Gia further. If she found no skeletons in his closet, all the better. But if she found some, at least Gia would know the facts.

Minutes later Kat stood on the opposite side of the ship, alone. The distance from Raphael made her almost forget all about him. She leaned against the railing and inhaled the salty sea air. Something about the ocean always washed her worries away.

She jumped as something splashed and broke through the water. It was a pod of killer whales a hundred feet away. They breached and sprayed misty water as they circled each other playfully, oblivious to her and the ship.

The whales frolicked as they breeched higher and higher. Circular waves expanded outwards as they played. They were beautiful, so carefree and wild.

She considered calling the others, but decided against it. The whales would disappear soon enough. She would just enjoy them before the spell was broken. It was nice to be alone with her thoughts for a while.

She didn't want to risk another altercation with Gia, either. They had known each other for so long that they practically read each other's minds. Time apart gave them a chance to calm down.

The whales disappeared from view as the yacht motored past them. *The Financier* had crossed the Juan de Fuca Strait and was expected to arrive at De Courcy within the hour.

Her alone time also gave her an opportunity to dig up a little information on her own. She strolled laps around the deck as a ruse to run into one of the crew without Raphael or the others noticing.

A casual conversation with crew members might be a way to glean further information on Raphael's background. For starters, she could determine how and when he got his yacht. An innocent-sounding question that could either validate or discredit his claims, and might also provide further information on his background. Gia's information was too sparse to evaluate what she had gotten herself into. Her love-struck friend apparently didn't even care to find out more.

Ten laps later, Kat still hadn't seen a soul. Wherever the crew was, it wasn't on deck. All she could show for her efforts were sweat-soaked clothes and a parched throat. She sighed and headed for the stairs and the comfort of her air-conditioned stateroom.

"Arggh!" She rounded the corner and ran smack into a wiry blond-haired man. The unshaven man wore frayed shorts and a stained t-shirt. He looked more like a drug addict than a crew member, definitely out of place on the luxurious *Financier*. He also smelled like he hadn't bathed in a week. He also seemed intent on avoiding her, no small feat since they had just collided.

"Sorry." He quickly averted his eyes and stepped aside.

"Wait a sec—you're part of the crew, aren't you?" While she hadn't expected Raphael's employees to sport uniforms, she figured they would at least look presentable. And look her in the eye. This guy did neither, which gave her an uneasy feeling.

"Yeah." He stepped back and turned to leave.

"Must be fascinating to work aboard a state-of-the-art vessel like this." *The Financier* had everything: the latest technology for navigation as well as leading-edge electronics in their staterooms. She glanced up at the small camera mounted above them. Naturally a yacht this size had a surveillance system.

He shrugged. "It's a job."

A strange answer. She'd bet that most sailors would kill to work on such a luxurious, hi-tech vessel. "You don't have an Italian accent. Did you just get hired?" He didn't look Italian, either. Judging by his clothing and unaccented English, he might even be local.

His face reddened. "I gotta go."

"Must be nice, sailing all over the world." Kat blocked his path and smiled. Her efforts to spark a conversation proved futile.

"I wouldn't know 'bout that." He turned his head as if looking for someone. "I just started a couple weeks ago."

"You haven't sailed with Raphael long, then?"

"Not really." He looked momentarily confused. "Like I said, I just got hired." He turned to leave.

Sailing from Italy meant a lot of open water and few ports to hire new crew. "Where did you join the crew?"

The man ignored her. He pretended to inspect the railing as he backed away.

"Wait—what's your name?"

He paused, appearing uncertain. "Pete."

"Nice to meet you, Pete. I'm Kat." She held out her hand.

After an awkward moment, Pete stepped forward to shake her hand. "I really gotta go now. Shouldn't be standing around. I got work to do."

"I guess you're taking us to De Courcy Island?" Though she had spent all her life in Vancouver, she hadn't even heard of De Courcy Island until Jace mentioned it. Not surprising, considering the island's limited access by private boat or plane. There were just a few dozen homes there and no facilities. Groceries and supplies had to be brought onto the island by boat.

He chuckled softly. "That I am."

"You know the legend about Brother XII and the Aquarian Foundation?"

"That's the cult, right?" Pete kicked at an imaginary rock at his feet on the spotless deck.

Kat nodded. "There's rumors of slave labor, too. People got tricked into handing their money over once they reached the island. They separated husbands and wives, forcing them to work long hours."

"Some of that's probably exaggerated." Pete's face darkened. "Over the years I've heard black magic, occultism, and such. Mostly made-up stories."

Words that applied equally to Raphael, she thought. Pete knew the story. He must be local.

"Hard to know for sure," Kat agreed. "I'm sure the story's been embellished over the years." She made a note to ask Jace.

"Probably."

"That Brother XII guy—I heard he took everyone's money as soon as they arrived. Kind of like it was communal property or something," Kat said. "Except that he used all the money himself. The Aquarian Foundation paid for the property, but all the property deeds were issued in his name."

Pete smiled. "That's what they say. There's also a rumor of buried treasure somewhere on the island. Treasure hunters have searched over the years, but always come up empty. Jars of gold are supposed to be buried underground, though no one's ever found any."

"That sounds fascinating. I'd love to know more."

Kat couldn't wait to explore the island. She wanted to do a little research on the mysterious Brother XII herself. But for now her focus remained on Raphael. Now that she had broken the ice with Pete, he might open up about how he had come to be on Raphael's yacht in the first place. That could provide a starting point to investigate Raphael himself. Gia trusted him, but she didn't.

"Later." He nodded and disappeared around the corner.

She spent the next few minutes scanning the horizon. They were surrounded by islands, though she couldn't identify any of them. She wondered why Brother XII had chosen this place for his cult. It wasn't easy to get to. Of course, that also made it harder to leave.

She turned her thoughts back to Pete and wondered how he and Raphael had even met. Probably at a local marina, but why had Raphael hired local crew for his live-aboard Italian yacht? Crew normally traveled with the vessel, wherever it went.

Maybe one of the Italian crew had quit or got fired, but that seemed unlikely in a foreign country so far from home. Scruffy-looking Pete seemed like a last resort choice for crew, especially for a billionaire. Billionaires usually screened and vetted their employees, especially those on their live-aboard yacht. At a minimum, they had a professional appearance. Pete didn't fit the bill.

Aside from Raphael's rag-tag skeleton crew and his security cameras, there was no security on board the vessel. She had expected at least a bodyguard. Few billionaires left themselves so vulnerable and unguarded on the unpatrolled open seas.

Pete just might hold a piece of the puzzle to unlock Raphael's true intentions. If only she could get him to talk.

She turned to go and almost collided with Harry. The corner was apparently a high accident area. Raphael really needed to install a mirror or something.

Pete suddenly reappeared behind him.

Harry pointed starboard. "Land ahoy!"

Pete followed behind him and burst into laughter. "Haven't heard that in a long time."

"You got the best job in the world," Harry said. "Second to your boss, of course. How long have you worked for Raphael?"

"A few weeks," Pete said. "I'm here till the end of the month, like the other guys."

Kat hadn't even considered that Pete might be temporary. Even if Raphael was docking his yacht, he couldn't completely abandon it without crew, especially since it was his residence.

What happened at month-end to cause Raphael to dismiss his crew? She almost didn't want to know.

Leave it to Harry. Within a minute he had the lowdown without prying at all. The entire crew was new, which confirmed that Raphael had probably lied about sailing from Italy. He certainly needed a full crew complement for longer than a few weeks if he planned to return to Italy.

Raphael wasn't likely to admit much, but she planned to pry more out of Pete. Maybe Raphael didn't even own the boat. He could have easily chartered it. That theory made sense if the crew was leaving at the end of the month.

But if Pete was gone at the end of the month, Raphael probably was, too. That put zero-hour at less than two weeks. Of course she was jumping to conclusions because she had no proof of any wrongdoing. Just a hunch.

If Raphael already had Gia's money, he could disappear at any time. Unless he wanted more money. She had no idea how much Gia had already invested, but it took a small fortune for the yacht's daily operation alone. Even if Gia had invested everything she had, it would barely cover Raphael's expenses. He was probably scheming to get more money. Either that or she was completely wrong about the guy. Raphael could be completely legitimate as Gia claimed.

Pete opened a storage box and lifted lifejackets out.

"Let me help you." Harry joined in and the two men piled the lifejackets on deck beside the storage box.

"What'll you do when you're done?" Harry asked.

"Dunno. I guess I'll look for another job."

"On a boat?"

Pete sighed. "That would be nice, but it's pretty tough finding work right now. This came up at the last minute."

Kat's ears perked up. Work shortages meant tough competition for the few jobs available, and Pete hardly looked like a top-level candidate. "How did you find out about this job?"

Pete frowned. "I heard about it."

Her question had made him suspicious. Harry was much better at casual questions than she was. Probably because he wasn't fishing for answers in the first place, like she was. "From where? Someone you knew?"

Pete motioned with his arm. "We're almost at the island. You'd better grab your stuff and get ready."

Kat stole a glance at Harry, hoping he'd pick up on her questions.

He didn't miss a beat. "This the nicest yacht you've ever worked on?"

Pete nodded. "It's the only one I've worked on. It's been worth it just to get back here."

"Back from where?" Harry asked. "You go away somewhere?"

"Gotta get back to work." Pete practically knocked Harry over in his haste to get away. "This ship's not gonna dock herself."

As Pete disappeared around the corner, Kat puzzled over his comment. Pete implied that he was local. And unlike Raphael, he seemed familiar with De Courcy Island. Back from where, exactly? She intended to find out.

Chapter 6

Kat entered her stateroom, anticipating a cool, refreshing shower.

Jace was already inside. He shoved clothes into his backpack on the bed.

"Going somewhere?"

"Raphael and I are exploring the island. We're going to see what's left of the old Brother XII settlement."

"I'll shower and change and grab my stuff." She untwisted her ponytail and rifled through her bag for a change of clothes.

Silence.

She turned around and glanced at Jace.

He fidgeted with his hands as he sat on the bed. He stared down at his hiking boots instead of meeting her gaze.

Kat swallowed as a lump caught in her throat. Had he planned to leave without her? "Oh, I see. I guess I'm not invited?"

"I-uh, figured you had already planned something with Gia. Or maybe Harry." Jace slung his pack over his shoulder and stood. "There's lots to do on board. Or you guys might want to beachcomb or something."

"But we planned to check out the island together, Jace." Before you replaced me with Raphael, she thought. Was she jealous, or suspicious? It felt a little like both.

"I thought it would be more efficient this way, especially since I'm doing two stories in one. I can interview Raphael while we walk to the Brother XII site." He turned towards the door. "You and I can visit on our own later on."

Kat frowned. "I see where this is going. You don't want me to go."

"Don't be silly. If you're quick you can come with us." He walked to the door, then turned around. "Just meet us up on deck."

Tears stung her eyes. Jace really didn't want her there. He denied it, but there was no question that he'd rather keep her and Raphael apart. She kind of understood his preoccupation and fascination with Raphael. It wasn't every day he met a billionaire, but that was beside the point. Their weekend getaway had morphed into a group thing with zero time alone.

She avoided his gaze and stared out the porthole. They idled just outside the marina. There were only two boats docked, a fishing dinghy and a beat-up trawler. The marina seemed very small for *The Financier.*

Her heart beat faster. "Aside from your assignment, this was supposed to be our weekend away. But you'd rather spend time with Raphael than me. I get it. I'm not a flashy billionaire with expensive toys. I'm just your girlfriend." Maybe she was overacting but at this point she didn't care. A few hours into the weekend and she just wanted to turn around and go home.

"That's not what I meant, Kat." Jace stood in the open doorway and rolled his eyes. "Of course I'd rather spend my time with you. But this is a big story opportunity. I can get two articles in one day. You're the one that suggested I do an article on him, so why are you making such a big deal about it? If I'm going to write about the guy, I need to talk to him first."

"You don't need to spend every waking moment with him."

Jace threw his hands up in the air. "We've only been aboard a few hours. We've still got all weekend. Besides, he's a really busy guy and might have to take off somewhere. I don't know how long he'll be around."

"Not long, I hope." He wouldn't stick around once she exposed him. That was certain.

"You seem to think he's a criminal or something. I think you're interested in my story just so that you can investigate the facts."

Silence.

"I'm right, aren't I?"

"It wouldn't hurt to find out a bit more about his background. Some of his claims seem a bit unbelievable. You'll have to verify them no matter what."

Harry walked past the open door and waved. "You two coming upstairs?"

Jace shook his head.

Harry glanced first at Jace and then Kat. His smile vanished and so did he.

Jace turned and closed the door behind him. He sat on the bed beside Kat. "Why are we arguing about this? We should be enjoying ourselves."

"Because you'd rather be with him than me." It sounded stupid when she said it aloud, but it was the truth.

"No I wouldn't." He pulled her close and kissed her. "I'd rather you came with us, but I'm worried you'll lose your temper with Raphael. You can't say anything confrontational or embarrassing."

"Oh, so now I'm an embarrassment?" Tears stung her eyes. No way was she going to cry. She turned away and sucked in her breath. She was entitled to her own opinions about Raphael. Couldn't she express them without being shunned?

"You know what I mean. I think you're being a little overprotective of Gia, but you've really got to keep your suspicions to yourself. Their relationship is none of our business. I happen to think he's totally legit, even if you don't. Besides, he brought us all the way here. We should at least be polite to him."

Jace might be right. At least about the keeping suspicions to herself part. She would hold her temper in check, but she wouldn't hold back while he stole from her friend. More than ever she had to investigate Raphael's background. She just wouldn't tell anybody about it. Especially not Jace.

Chapter 7

Kat needn't have rushed. When she emerged on deck fifteen minutes later, they still hadn't docked. *The Financier* was too large for the tiny De Courcy Island marina, so they had to relocate. The yacht anchored off Pirate's Cove instead.

"Pete says we'll take the dinghy to the island." Uncle Harry's eyes narrowed as he studied her. "You look like you're in a bad mood."

"I'm fine." She wasn't and couldn't hide it from Harry. Thankfully he didn't press her further.

"If you say so, but you don't look happy to me. I'm going to see what this dinghy-thingy is all about." He laughed at his own joke and disappeared in the direction of the bow.

She took a deep breath and exhaled. Jace was right. How hard was it to just grin and bear Raphael's company for a couple of days? It was the weekend and they were anchored off a sparsely populated island.

In fact, De Courcy Island was an ideal place to be. It bought her time to uncover Raphael's secrets. Close quarters on a yacht was a perfect way to keep tabs on him, something that would have been impossible back in Vancouver. She was confident that once she exposed his true character and secrets, everyone would listen to what she had to say.

Harry returned in less than ten minutes. "I wish Raphael and Gia would hurry up. Can't we just go ashore without them?"

"They shouldn't be much longer," Kat said. Gia had mentioned a conference call with Raphael's investors in Italy, but it should have ended a half-hour ago.

"I'm dying to get there too, but think we'd better wait," Jace said. "It's hard to believe a commune ever existed on this tiny island. So many people lived here, yet they're largely forgotten."

"Or that so many people got tricked into handing all their money over to Brother XII," Kat said.

Jace cast a wary glance at Kat. "That guy had enough charisma to sell a new religion to the Pope. He convinced more than 8,000 people to follow him by seducing them with his tales of mysticism and reincarnation."

"That's what happens when you say the world's going to end," Harry said. "People lose their common sense."

"Brother XII promised a way out. The world would end for the masses, but not the elite few chosen to join the Aquarian Foundation. Anyone who joined the cult was promised a better outcome. His followers grew as newspapers spread stories about his ability to foresee the future."

"People believe what they want to," Kat said. "They think that if they put their faith in a higher power, destiny is out of their hands. That way they can absolve themselves of any blame."

Jace nodded. "Some people were taken advantage of more than others. Aside from the publishers who shared Brother XII's message, he convinced Mary Connally, a wealthy widow from Asheville, North Carolina, that he held the secret to divine help and spiritual redemption. Connally sent him $2,000, saying she had more funds available."

"Boy, this guy really knows how to trick people." Harry shook his head. "Why did she believe him?"

"It was hard not to. Brother XII took a train to Toronto and met her in person. But on the train he met Mrs. Myrtle Baumgartner. He convinced her that she was the reincarnated Egyptian god of fertility, Isis."

"A sucker's born every minute," quipped Uncle Harry.

Jace nodded. "By the end of the three-day train trip, he had also convinced her that they were destined to be together. He was the reincarnation of Osiris, husband of Isis."

"She was already married, though." Kat frowned.

"Apparently he made such an impression on Myrtle that she waited for his return. She was so enthralled with him that when he did, she eventually left her husband and family to join the Aquarian Foundation."

Uncle Harry shook his head. "How could anyone believe something so far-fetched?"

"Brother XII was very convincing because many people fell for his claims. While in Toronto he got almost $26,000 and a pledge of devotion from Mary Connally. That was a lot of money back then. And don't forget—he was still married. This was the final straw, though. His wife Alma had enough and finally left her husband. Less than a week later, Brother XII brought Myrtle to live with him."

"Creepy guy," Harry said. "He was so good at getting other people's money that I wonder if there's any left on the island."

Jace leaned against the railing. "I doubt it. But you never know."

"I'm surprised people didn't wise up," Uncle Harry said. "Wasn't it obvious they were being cheated?"

"People usually don't realize it until it's too late," Kat said. "Brother XII simply told them what they wanted to hear. They wanted to think that they were not only special but also part of something big. That somehow, they mattered more than other people did. It boosted their egos and blinded them to whatever else was going on. It worked like a charm."

"It definitely does," Jace agreed. "Brother XII kept all their money for himself, and put everybody to work like slaves. He separated the men and the women, husbands and wives, and worked them sixteen to eighteen hours a day with very little rest."

"You have to be crazy to do that." Uncle Harry shook his head. "I'd never fall for anything like that."

"You'd be surprised, Uncle Harry," Kat said. "You're on an island, separated from the rest of society and isolated from the world. You've got no money, no possessions and no way of getting off the island. You're basically at the mercy of the person feeding you. Ironically, that person is buying the food with your money. But it's not your money anymore. You've lost control of everything you owned."

"That's exactly what happened," Jace said. "Brother XII claimed there weren't enough spaces for everybody in the commune. Everyone competed in a trial to see who would make the cut. Only the chosen few would get refuge in the city they were building."

"And the rest?" Kat asked.

"Anyone remaining outside the city would die, or at least that's what they thought. It was their only chance for survival, so they were willing to do anything to be the chosen ones. Maybe it was crazy, but after a few months or years, everything seemed normal to them. Since no one came or went off the islands, they had no outside influence. No one challenged them on their beliefs."

"You said they competed," Uncle Harry said. "Who won?"

"Nobody." Jace sighed. "Everybody lost something. Some more than others."

Gulls shrieked and pierced the silence overhead. Kat, Jace, and Harry stood silent as they gazed at De Courcy Island. So much tragedy and heartbreak, yet today not a trace remained.

"I'd be in denial too after making such a big mistake," Harry said. "As long as you pretended everything was fine, you never faced the truth that you were an idiot. Those people gave up all their hard-earned money and ruined their own lives. Brother XII helped them, but it was their stupid decision in the first place."

"Yeah," Jace agreed. "Hindsight is 20/20. Even then, not everyone wants to see the truth."

Kat glanced towards the door. "What are Gia and Raphael doing, anyway? What kind of business meeting are they having?"

Jace shot her a warning look.

She checked her watch. It was almost three p.m. local time. "In Italy it's almost midnight. Who could they possibly be talking to so late on a Friday night?"

"Billionaires don't keep normal office hours," Jace said. "But I wish they'd hurry up, too. I can't wait to set foot on the island. You know, some people call this a treasure island. Rumor has it that Brother XII hid a half-ton of gold coins here."

The gold again. Just like Pete mentioned.

"Pete said Brother XII kept the gold coins in Mason jars." Harry recounted Pete's comments. "Where did he get all that money?"

"The donations to the Aquarian Foundation were all made in cash," Jace said. "Brother XII converted all that into gold. Since he had such an uncanny ability to handpick wealthy members, all their worldly assets amounted to a tidy sum. At least one of his followers was a millionaire, so the money added up quickly."

"Why not just put it in the bank?" Harry scratched his chin thoughtfully. "That would be much easier, wouldn't it?"

"Easy maybe, but bank transactions leave a paper trail. Gold doesn't. Unlike money in the bank, it was untraceable with no transaction records. It was pretty ingenious of him. He could spend the money without anyone knowing. There was also no evidence of payment from the donors, so they couldn't prove they had given it to him in the first place if problems arose. Of course, that was his plan all along, to take the money for himself."

"That's crazy," Kat said. "They should have known better. They were wealthy people. What did their financial advisors say?"

"There was no stopping them, no matter what their advisors told them. They were entranced with Brother XII's claims that he could foretell the future. In hindsight, of course, they regretted it when the white magic turned into black magic.

"They handed over all their money because they believed everything he told them. He encouraged them to come and settle on the island. They built houses and invested everything they had to buy the land underneath. Yet they never got a property deed. Brother XII got the deeds instead. He claimed it was all a communal project, so there would be no individual ownership."

"Why didn't his followers just wise up?" Uncle Harry asked. "It must have been obvious after a while."

"Not really. No one even knew where the gold was kept. So as far as they knew, it remained the property of the Aquarian Foundation and was still hidden and untouched."

"But if he took their money and gave nothing in return, sooner or later they should've figured it all out," Uncle Harry said.

"That's where it gets interesting," Jace said. "He convinced them that their souls would be destroyed. They wouldn't be reincarnated. In addition they risked being left out of the refuge, since there were more people than spaces available. Only the chosen few would be given sanctuary during Armageddon, and if they protested, plenty of others were happy to take their places."

Raphael and Gia finally appeared. Gia smiled apologetically. "We're ready to go ashore now. Sorry about the wait."

Gia gave no further explanation.

"Tell me more about this half-ton of gold," Harry said. "Is there a treasure map?"

Jace laughed. "Not that I know of. But rumor has it that Brother XII buried the gold right here on the island."

The treasure talk piqued Raphael's interest. "Why would he do that?"

"To escape scrutiny and keep it close at hand. That's the focus of my story." Jace pointed to the island. "The Aquarian Foundation bought De Courcy Island and a couple of others in the spring of 1929, after the cult had been going for a few years. Whenever people started to ask questions, he moved the group to more isolated locations."

Kat forgot her distaste of Raphael as she got caught up in the moment. "The roaring twenties were about to end. It was just months before the stock market crash of 1929 and the start of the Great Depression."

"That's right," Jace said. "Though the stock market was booming, lots of people expected a crash sooner or later. All the signs were there—the jittery financial markets in Europe and here in North America, and a disparity of wealth between the rich and poor."

"Why would anyone choose to live here?" Gia asked. "It's pretty and all, but it's small and in the middle of nowhere. You need a boat or you're stranded."

"That's precisely why Brother XII liked it. It shielded him from prying eyes. People had started to speculate about his motives. He went after the wealthy, and his rich followers grew when he predicted the stock market crash. To them, it proved that he could foretell the future, including Armageddon. People saw the islands as a refuge from the financial strife and turbulent financial markets."

"I guess all those rich investors thought they'd get more money in a future life." Harry laughed. "Like that would ever happen."

"And the nearest bank was miles away by boat." Raphael stroked his chin. "So he buried the money to keep it secure."

"How did he get such power over people? You have to be pretty stupid to just hand over your money, right?" Gia looked at Raphael for confirmation, but he remained expressionless.

"Charisma," Jace said. "He also had them convinced he was a mystic with a direct connection to the gods. They were afraid of doing anything that endangered their souls' chance of survival when the end of the world came."

"Any normal person would see through that." Gia frowned. "All it takes is a bit of common sense."

Jace smiled. "You'd think so, but Brother XII had a few tricks up his sleeve. He retreated to what he called his House of Mystery where he held séances and he claimed he communicated directly with the other eleven brothers. He didn't allow anyone inside the House of Mystery, but he made his followers stand outside, sometimes for hours. He claimed their meditation helped him with astral projection and connecting with the other deities.

"His séances often lasted hours and people inevitably grew restless. Some gossiped, some complained. Yet somehow Brother XII always knew what was said outside and who said it. The doubters were always punished. In their eyes, he truly was a psychic. They lived in both fear and awe of him.

"What his followers didn't know was that Brother XII had secretly hired an electrician who installed microphones behind the rocks at the designated waiting area outside his house. It was cutting-edge technology at the time, not something many people were familiar with or would expect. All he had to do was listen."

Kat sighed. If only someone would listen to her.

Chapter 8

Kat stepped out of the dinghy and into knee-deep water, glad to finally be at the island. She glanced back at *The Financier* as she walked towards the rocky beach. Even from a distance the yacht looked massive.

Raphael dragged the dinghy far enough onto the beach that it wouldn't get caught and pulled out by the tide. The men had already forgotten her presence. Jace talked about Brother XII and Raphael hung on his every word.

She paused for a moment and then fell in behind Jace and Raphael. She trailed several feet behind the men as they crossed the beach. It was enough to distance herself from Raphael, yet still hear their conversation. Her strategy ensured she kept her cool.

Gia and Harry had remained behind on *The Financier*. Gia was tired and Harry's back was acting up again. Kat had also debated staying behind, but she hadn't come all this way to miss whatever remained of Brother XII's world. Besides, she believed in the old Chinese proverb of keeping her friends close and her enemies closer.

It was now almost 4 p.m. Raphael still hadn't explained the reason for the conference call with his Italian investors, only that it somehow involved Gia. Yet Gia remained evasive when Kat pressed for details.

Gia was furious that Kat had even questioned the authenticity of Raphael and his company. Kat figured she probably had it coming, but she couldn't just sit back and watch her friend get both jilted and swindled.

With Gia barely speaking to her, it was difficult to get any details about Gia's agreement with Raphael. In trying to protect her friend, she had instead alienated her. In fact, everything she said just angered Gia more. Not that she blamed her. But there were things that had to be said, if only to stop Gia's disaster from unfolding.

She paused momentarily on the rocky beach and imagined how a new commune member must have felt when they arrived on shore. They had given up all their possessions and arrived on a desolate island far removed from the outside world.

Kat looked forward to seeing the remnants of Brother XII's abandoned settlement. Cults had always fascinated her. Reasonable people were somehow brainwashed into surrendering their possessions and more importantly, their free will. The Aquarian Foundation was a perfect example. There was good reason it was mostly forgotten today. People probably wanted to forget and put such unfortunate events behind them.

"What are we waiting for? Let's go," Raphael said.

They headed uphill on a trail that led inland. The path paralleled the rocky cliffs, partially shaded by wiry arbutus trees that clung to the rocks. Gradually the arbutus trees transitioned to taller pine trees as they traveled further inland from the shore. The path leveled out and dappled sun turned to cool shade, a refreshing change.

"Tell me about your business. How did it start?" Jace asked.

Raphael nodded. "Mama had a salon back home in Milan. As a small boy I used to play there and even though I was young, I noticed how she transformed plain-looking women into glamor queens. She wasn't so good at the financial side of the business. Her talents were inventing new styles and hair products. Soon she attracted the attention of Italian movie stars and models. As a matter of fact, Gia reminds me a lot of Mama."

"Really? How?" Jace asked.

"She knows her customers and also what sells. She's not afraid to take calculated risks."

That was news to Kat. The Gia she knew was ultra-cautious, postponing her salon renovations until her profits increased. What had changed with Raphael?

She remained silent in order to glean as much information from Raphael as she could. She followed the men to a small rock outcropping that also marked a fork in the trail. They headed right.

"Does your mother still operate her salon?" Jace asked.

"Hell, no." Raphael laughed. The dirt path made a slight incline as it led further into the forest. "She doesn't need to lift a finger for the rest of her life. We are now very wealthy thanks to Bellissima. Now Mama is the one getting beauty treatments."

Jace chuckled. "And you helped her get there."

"I took care of the business side, with marketing and venture capital to finance the manufacturing and product development. But the idea, the word of mouth and celebrity endorsement was all Mama's work. That's something money can't buy."

"You're just being modest," Jace said.

Jace had taken no time at all in joining the Raphael fan club. Where was his journalistic skepticism and neutrality?

"What's the name of your company, Raphael?" The words slipped before Kat could stop herself. With all the talk of his success, he was awfully short on details.

No answer.

He had almost certainly heard her, so she didn't repeat the question. Jace didn't seem to notice Raphael's selective hearing, or if he did, he didn't comment.

Moments later they arrived at the settlement. Raphael regained his voice as talk turned to Brother XII and the Aquarian Foundation. Not much was left of the site, other than faint impressions of where buildings had once stood.

Jace pointed to the remnants of a cement foundation the size of several houses. "That must be where the schoolhouse was," he said. "They built it because they expected students, but none came. Most of the disciples were middle-aged or older, so there weren't any children."

"Maybe that was a good thing," Kat said. "Imagine being born into a cult. You wouldn't know any different."

Jace nodded. "Brainwashed from birth. Hard to undo that."

"This is all there is?" Raphael kicked at the dirt with his foot. "I thought there would be restored buildings and stuff."

"Where's the House of Mystery?" Kat scanned the ground for another building outline that would be grander than most. "Oh, I think I see it." The faint remains of a building foundation stood on a small knoll that overlooked the settlement. Where he could keep an eye on his subjects, she thought.

"How long did this cult exist?" Raphael asked. "They seem to have moved around a lot."

"Just a few years," Jace said. "Even his most die-hard followers became disillusioned when his promises of a new age didn't materialize. They eventually saw through some of his claims."

"It's not exactly easy to get here." Raphael scanned the landscape. "And it's on a rocky island. You couldn't be self-sufficient here. What's so great about this place?"

"Brother XII liked the fact it was away from prying eyes. He didn't want to attract attention because that invited questions. And the questions weren't just from outsiders. The Aquarian Foundation members wanted to know why he could live with Myrtle while still married to Alma. That sort of behavior was scandalous at the time. Or why the property titles were registered to him personally instead of in the Foundation's name.

"But even more questionable was why the followers worked so hard in what amounted to forced labor for no pay. Many were senior citizens who practically worked themselves to death. They were little more than his slaves."

Kat stared at the foundation outlines, some of which were overgrown with vegetation. It was like an archaeological site. One that people would rather forget. "I still can't believe the people chose to stay here. I guess they were destitute by then, and probably too mentally and physically exhausted to escape."

"And too afraid," Jace added. "They still believed that Brother XII had power over them. They feared the consequences if they left. Even if his spiritual claims were false, where would they go? They had alienated their families when they turned over their wealth to Brother XII. Or in the case of some of the women, abandoned their husbands for Brother XII's affections. Most were from other countries. They had no means or money to get back home.

"There was a bit of a reprieve from their back-breaking labor and hard scrabble existence when Brother XII and his current lover, Madame Zee, left for England in 1930, sailing away in a trawler complete with gun turrets for defense.

"They were gone for almost two years, long enough for people to realize their mistake. They banded together and confronted Brother XII upon his return. He banished the more vocal protestors, but it was the beginning of the end. One way or another, his followers were able to finally leave the island. Once they reached the outside world they realized the extent of their losses. In 1933, several followers sued to freeze the Aquarian Foundation assets and get their money back.

"They were only partially successful, since Brother XII had done a good job of hiding the assets. The gold couldn't be traced and he had already spent a lot of the money on himself. Mary Connally recouped some of her money when the De Courcy and Valdes property deeds were transferred into her name as partial compensation.

"Brother XII at least foresaw his own demise, and he left the settlement in a hurry with Madame Zee." He shook his head. "But not before burning all the buildings down. He took an axe to the furniture and ruined everything just so that no one else could use it."

"What about the money?" Raphael asked.

"The gold?" Jace shrugged. "Some say it's buried here on the island, that he didn't have time to retrieve it. But I doubt that."

Raphael's mouth dropped open. "How much did he get away with?"

"No one really knows. Most people were ashamed to admit they had invested, let alone the amount they had been cheated out of. Since they had all been wealthy when they joined, it had to be a tidy sum." Jace paused. "There's another rumor, about a cave on the island. Some think Brother XII hid some of the gold treasure there."

"What are we waiting for?" Raphael turned towards the trail. "Let's go."

Kat trailed behind the two men as they left the settlement behind. They returned to the trail but took a separate fork that lead behind the clearing. The trail's cool shade was lush and refreshing, lined with salmonberry bushes and knee-high vegetation. It was a sharp contrast from the barren and windswept oceanfront cliffs.

Less than a hundred feet later the path ascended up a steep hill. Kat's still-wet feet slid in her flip-flops and she grabbed branches and plants to stay on her feet. She wished she had worn sturdier footwear.

Jace led the way, followed by Raphael. She struggled to keep pace as the gap between her and Raphael widened to ten feet, then twenty.

"Slow down a bit," she said as her right foot slipped out of her flip-flop.

Raphael either didn't hear or chose to ignore her. She regained her footing and closed the gap.

"Tell me more about your mom," Jace said.

"Mama gained quite a reputation and women flocked to her salon from miles away. She soon attracted the attention of a large Italian beauty supply company. Mama licensed the secret formula to them and the rest is history." Raphael paused on the trail and turned around to face Kat.

"Licensing was a smart move," Kat said. "Most people would have sold their invention outright." It bordered on unbelievable that in this day and age, Raphael's mother had developed a new hair product outside of a chemistry lab. But she played along. Any answer Raphael gave would be fabricated, but sooner or later he would slip up and reveal something.

"Mama didn't sell her formula because she wanted to keep creative control," Raphael said. "That part worked out quite well."

Raphael's selective hearing was working again.

"Is she working on any new products?"

Raphael didn't answer.

They paused in the clearing. Two paths led in opposite directions with no signs or markings.

"Oh, the stories I could tell about some of these celebrities." Raphael made a zipping motion across his lips. "But naturally my lips are sealed." He listed off a dozen film stars and celebrities who endorsed Bellissima. "All the biggest European names and soon the biggest North American stars too."

"Smart lady," Jace said. "Kat, maybe you should try his hair products out."

Kat scowled. "Why? What's wrong with my hair the way it is?" Why did everyone think her hair needed fixing?

"Not saying you need it, but you're the only person here with curly hair. It would make an interesting experiment. Do you have any product on board, Raphael?"

Raphael laughed. "I'm afraid not. Sorry to disappoint you, but Kat's hair will have to stay the way it is for now."

She ignored the insult. "You don't carry it around with you?" No product meant there was no danger of her being experimented on. And no danger of being exposed as a fake. Only a scammer would avoid having products on hand for demonstration and promotion.

"I've run out of product," Raphael said. "I won't have more until next week."

Kat sidestepped a large tree root. Raphael couldn't gain customers without product. Yet he had tricked Gia into investing without even trying Bellissima.

"I suppose your manufacturer takes care of all your distribution?" Jace asked.

"Exactly." Raphael waved his arm. "They manage all the logistics. We sign up the authorized retailers and hand the manufacturing and distribution off to them. No one can copy our patented formula."

Jace raised his brows. "Sweet deal. No wonder you have time to travel around on your yacht."

"What's to stop anyone from reverse engineering the formula?" Kat asked. Dozens of Chinese factories unlocked complex formulas every day. If Raphael's product was as revolutionary and profitable as he claimed, there would be no shortage of imitators and counterfeiters looking to get in on the action.

Raphael ignored her, as expected.

The tree cover was denser and the air more humid. She paused to admire a waterfall, partly to keep her temper in check. She sighed as the men's voices faded.

Just as well. She was tired of hearing about Raphael's larger than life successes. Not just because they were lies, but also because she couldn't stand to see normally objective Jace fall under Raphael's spell.

She gathered her thoughts for a few moments. As the forest fell silent, she suddenly realized she couldn't hear the men's voices anymore. She'd better catch up to the men.

"I'm right behind you," Kat called to Jace and Raphael ahead of her.

No one answered.

She was mad that Jace hadn't noticed her falling behind.

She debated turning around and heading back to the beach, especially because it was difficult to keep pace in her flip-flops. She decided to carry on since she had come all this way to see the settlement and the cave. The settlement had been a disappointment, but the cave might be better. She wasn't leaving until she saw it.

Kat trudged along in silence, taking her time. There was only one trail, so the danger of getting lost was unlikely. She winced as she felt a blister forming on her right foot. Next time she'd choose better footwear.

She bent down to adjust her flip-flop and was startled by a man's voice.

Chapter 9

Kat spun around and faced Pete. He sat on a tree stump several feet away and regarded her with a smirk.

"You won't get far in shoes like that." Raphael's meek crew member was suddenly full of confidence and sarcasm.

"You all alone?"

Kat fought back a general sense of unease. Pete seemed okay, but what did she really know about him? Nothing, other than he was a transient worker hired by an almost-certain scammer.

He stood and took a few steps towards her.

A scent of stale sweat and grime wafted towards her and she recoiled. She retreated a few feet but stumbled on the uneven ground. Her flip-flops slid sideways out from under her feet. Her ankle twisted as she fought to regain her balance, but she lost. She collapsed in a heap and rolled down the side of the trail bank.

She looked up and saw Pete standing above her. "Thanks. I'm okay."

"Relax. I'm harmless." Pete held out his hand and helped her to her feet. "Probably not a good idea to wander off by yourself though. You might get lost or something."

"I'm not alone. Raphael and Jace are up ahead." She bent over and brushed the dirt off her knees and feet. Her ankle throbbed and she shook it out as she grabbed a tree trunk for balance.

Pete seemed surprised. "No, they turned back. They passed right by here a couple of minutes ago."

"I didn't see them. They weren't very far ahead of me, either. Where did they go?" It must have been when she had veered off the trail, yet she hadn't heard them pass.

Pete shrugged. "Back to the ship, I guess."

"We—I'm—headed to the cave. They were too. They couldn't have come and gone already."

He scratched his chin thoughtfully. "I guess they changed their minds once they saw it."

She waited for him to elaborate but he didn't. "I'm headed in the right direction, aren't I?" It surprised her that Jace hadn't spent at least a few minutes exploring.

"Yeah." He nodded. "It's just a few minutes further on the trail."

"Okay, well I'd better get going. I want to see where Brother XII hid his gold."

"You and a thousand other people." He chuckled. "There is no gold. Everyone's looking for the wrong thing. There is another treasure, though."

"What kind of a treasure?"

"A secret passage under the ocean. A subterranean tunnel that leads to another island."

"Wow. An actual tunnel under the ocean floor?"

He nodded. "Yeah. It's been used by the locals for thousands of years. It's like another world underground. It's incredible, but not many people know about it."

"How do you know so much about this place?" She had grown up on the mainland, close enough that she would surely have heard about something as fantastical as an underground passage. She hadn't, so she assumed it probably didn't exist. "Are you from around here?"

"Kind of. Grew up on another island. But that's another story." He furrowed his brows as he stared off into the distance. "You know anything about the cave?"

She shook her head. "What's so special about it?"

"It's three miles long and crosses under the ocean floor." He tilted his head in the direction she was headed. "The entrance is in the middle of the island, but if you go in far enough there's a drop off of a few hundred feet. The passage crosses under the water and comes out on Valdes Island across the strait."

"Really?" Jace would be fascinated, if he wasn't already under Raphael's influence. Another story that he had missed out on. She wasn't about to miss her opportunity, though. "Tell me more."

"The cave was used by the Coast Salish people as part of their ceremonial rites. The men fasted and then traveled through the undersea passage alone with only a single torch to guide them. They completed their mission by depositing their staffs in the sacred chamber and were celebrated when they completed the return trip back."

"Really? Have you hiked in there?" Was it hiking or spelunking? Probably the latter, since technically it was an underground cave.

Pete shook his head. "An earthquake more than a hundred years ago blocked the tunnel. It sealed in the sacred chamber, too. It's supposed to be full of archeological treasures, like ceremonial masks and staffs and stuff."

"If it's so amazing, why hasn't it been unblocked?" The secret chamber sounded like anthropologists' heaven. The skeptic in her thought it didn't connect at all. It was just an unsubstantiated legend.

"The boulders are the size of buildings," he said. "You'd need lots of heavy equipment. Maybe the cost's not worth it. Sometimes it's better to just leave things as they are."

"Unless Brother XII's gold is in there." Kat smiled. "At any rate, the cave sounds amazing. I can't wait to see it."

"Just be careful in there. You need to watch where you're going." He glanced at her feet. "You really shouldn't go by yourself."

He was right of course. "Can you show me?"

He shook his head. "I've got to get back to the ship."

It struck Kat as odd that Pete wouldn't return with them since he had swum ashore.

"I can show you tomorrow though."

"That would be great." As long as tomorrow wasn't too late. If Jace and Raphael weren't interested, they might not even remain at De Courcy another day. "I'll still walk to the entrance though. Might as well have a quick look before going back to the ship."

She thanked him and continued on the trail. Her ears perked up at the sound of running water and barely audible voices. But they were the voices of children, not Jace and Raphael.

Minutes later she encountered a family of four including a boy about ten and a girl around thirteen. She came within ten feet of them, close enough to hear them talking. The boy talked excitedly about the cave while the girl remained silent as she plucked ripe salmonberries from the bushes that lined the trail.

For reasons Kat couldn't quite explain, she veered off the trail again. She didn't feel like making small talk, so she followed the sound of running water to a small creek. She swatted a mosquito as she stopped by the stream. She bent down and ran her hand in the cold water. She drank it from her cupped hands and quenched her thirst. She shivered as she splashed her face and arms and rinsed sweat off her skin.

She waited a few feet off the trail until they passed. After their voices faded, new ones grew louder. Jace and Raphael hadn't returned to the ship as Pete had claimed. Either he was mistaken or had purposely lied.

She turned back towards the trail, intending to catch up with them. She scrambled up the bank and caught her foot on an exposed tree root. She lurched forward and landed on her side with a thud.

She grunted as she assessed the damage. Her ribcage pressed against the root-covered ground. She winced as she drew a breath inward. Was anything broken?

No.

After the shock of falling, she dusted off the pine needles and bark mulch and assessed the damage. A bit of blood from a skinned knee. Other than that she was unharmed.

She struggled to her feet. "Hey! Wait for me."

No answer.

She had only heard and not seen them, so it was hard to determine their direction of travel. Maybe they hadn't turned back at all. They could still be headed to the cave. In which case she could simply follow. She breathed a sigh of relief. She wouldn't be alone after all.

Odd that Pete had claimed to see them. He had probably seen others from afar and mistaken them for Jace and Raphael. Then again, the trail had passed within ten feet of Pete's vantage point. They were hard to miss unless Pete had vision problems.

She retraced her steps but the men's voices had already faded. They were headed towards the beach, in the opposite direction from the cave. They hadn't even waited for her.

Well, they would just have to wait for her at the beach instead. She wasn't boarding the dinghy without at least a glimpse of the cave. While Pete had offered to show her tomorrow, there were no guarantees they would still be moored at the island. Jace's assignment was the whole reason for being here, and if he wasn't interested in the cave, they probably wouldn't stick around.

Her ankle throbbed and she was angry that she had been left behind. More than anything, it bothered her that Jace hadn't even wondered where she was. Instead of worrying, he had completely forgotten about her.

She soon caught up with the family, despite her sore ankle. She slowed her pace, preferring solitude as her mood soured.

Their voices faded again as her distance from them widened. She stayed far enough back so that she could hear but not see them. Ten minutes was all she needed for a quick look at the cave so she could at least say she'd been there. A few minutes after that and she'd be back at the dinghy. Jace and Raphael could surely amuse themselves by talking about Raphael for at least that long.

Chapter 10

Kat had to turn sideways to slip through the cave entrance. It was little more than a crevice and she was immediately claustrophobic as she inhaled the dank, clammy air. Pete hadn't mentioned the narrow opening. She hesitated and fought the urge to leave.

She couldn't see or hear the family, but since the trail ended here, they must be inside the cave. She inched forward as her eyes adjusted to the darkness. At least the ground was level. She ran her hand along the smooth, damp walls that led in about twenty feet. Though the light barely penetrated the dark cave, it was clear that the cave led nowhere. She didn't see anything that resembled a tunnel.

She was about to exit when the cave wall gave way beneath her palm. On her right was an opening or alcove of sorts. She followed the wall's curve and stepped around the corner into a huge open cavern bathed in filtered sunlight. The contrast from a few feet away was stunning. Beams of light streamed from an opening at least thirty feet above her. Despite the open space, the air was even more humid than the dark passageway. Vines trailed down the damp cave walls and water droplets drizzled from above. At first she mistook the moisture for rain, but the mist was a result of the almost 100% humidity.

Somewhere in the distance water rushed, maybe a stream or a waterfall. She walked towards the sound, then hesitated. She really shouldn't venture further alone. Except she wasn't alone, since the family was ahead of her. If anything, it was better to catch up to them.

Jace and Raphael obviously knew she was here because she hadn't returned to the boat. Before long they would retrace their steps to search for her. Not that she wanted them to. She was still angry that they hadn't waited for her, or apparently even noticed her missing.

Whatever. She hadn't traveled here to miss all the attractions. She planned to at least explore the cave a little. She had time for a quick look before she headed back to the beach.

The water sound grew louder, and she imagined a waterfall cascading down rocks. The light dimmed as she ventured towards the melodic sound. It was a beautiful subterranean world even in darkness. She crossed the open area and was so mesmerized that she hit the rock barrier at full speed.

"Ouch!" her voice echoed through the cavern. Her nose throbbed from the impact. She had hit her nose and face on the rock.

She stepped back and lost her balance. She cursed as she tumbled to the ground. It was her second fall in just minutes.

"Hello?" Her voice echoed throughout the chamber as she pushed herself up onto her elbows. She wasn't even sure if she still faced the same direction. The darkness had enveloped her so quickly and completely that she was disoriented as to her direction of travel. How could she possibly retrace her steps if she didn't have her bearings? Her eyes should have adjusted to the darkness by now, yet she couldn't see a thing. Everything was black, with no hint of the open cavern she had traversed moments earlier. She fought rising panic and reminded herself to think clearly. All she had to do was feel around the cave wall in a methodical fashion to find the break in the cave wall. She could then retrace her steps to the entrance and the way out.

She hadn't heard the family's voices since entering the cave. Not even the children's' voices. The family must be further inside, probably lured by the same rushing water.

"Hello?" She hoped for a reassuring reply but heard only the echo of her own voice. Strange that she couldn't hear anyone.

She debated exploring further, but what more could she possibly discover in five or ten minutes? Venturing further just increased her risk of getting lost. Besides, now that she had found something, she could easily convince the whole group to return later to see the massive cavern. By then Uncle Harry's back might be better, and even Gia might be up for the trek. It was more fun to explore together.

Without a flashlight and proper shoes she wasn't equipped to go further anyway. She also hadn't seen any other lights inside the cave. Her pulse quickened as she wondered if the family had even entered the cave at all.

She rose to her knees and steadied herself. Her eyes adjusted to the darkness enough to make out a dim outline several feet away. It must be the cave wall. She counted her steps as she shuffled towards it. She breathed a sigh of relief when she touched the damp rock.

She leaned against the cave wall and assessed the damage. Her knee ached. In addition to being skinned, she had likely strained a ligament. Add in her sore ankle, and it was going to be a long, painful journey back to the beach. She rose slowly to a standing position and paused to test out her leg. She could walk as long as she avoided sudden turns.

She willed herself to remain calm and slid her palm along the cave wall. Within a minute she found the opening. But was it the same passageway? She hadn't considered that there could be multiple openings.

She turned the corner and emerged into another chamber. Her heart sank as she realized that it wasn't the same place. For one thing, the ground sloped downward and the ceiling was much lower, not more than ten feet high. This must be the start of the undersea tunnel.

She ventured further inside and it immediately darkened. She waited again for her eyes to adjust and soon made out dim outlines of the cave walls. As she took a few steps forward the ceiling dropped dramatically, to the point where her head almost touched it.

She continued on a slight downhill, but as she descended the ceiling gradually rose. A few minutes later the ground beneath her leveled out. She had no idea if she was still on the island or now under the sea. It was hard to be sure since she had made a few twists and turns. The only thing she was sure of was that she hadn't retraced her steps inland.

She kept her left hand on the cave wall to ensure she could retrace her steps back to the main chamber. It was amazing to think nature had created a tunnel under the sea. She had read somewhere that it was nearly impossible to build underground or even lay electrical cables in this part of the Pacific Ocean. The deep water and unstable ocean floor in an area prone to earthquakes had stumped engineers. Yet this natural tunnel had existed for thousands, or more likely millions of years. It had withstood earthquakes, storms, and possibly even the Ice Age.

She guessed she had been in the cave less than thirty minutes. Her confidence restored, she decided another five wouldn't hurt. She fingered the moist cave wall for reassurance and continued onward. A few more minutes and then she would reverse course and retrace her steps back to the entrance.

The water grew louder. It had to be a fairly substantial waterfall, one that Jace and Raphael had completely missed. That was another problem with Jace's Raphael obsession. In his quest to get another story, he had missed a chance of a lifetime to see a beautiful natural wonder. It was all the more disappointing since Jace loved the outdoors and they were unlikely to ever return here. The island was only accessible by private boat and they didn't own one. Jace had chased the bright shiny object and missed the treasure in plain sight. Judging by how quickly the guys had returned, they probably hadn't entered the cave at all.

She followed the water sound and emerged into a third cavern. This one was the largest yet, and much better lit. She stood before a pool about twenty feet wide. Turquoise green water cascaded into the pool from about eighty feet above her. Her mouth dropped open as she followed the waterfall upwards. The water's path had etched deep into the rock and carved a narrow canyon where the water spilled over the edge. From there it tumbled down into the pool before her.

The sheer size and rumble of the subterranean waterfall was breathtaking. Pete obviously hadn't known of its existence or he would have mentioned it. She gazed in awe and wondered if she was the first person to see it. Probably one of a chosen few and hopefully not the last.

The waterfall wasn't the only attraction. To the right of the water was a large flat boulder, probably ten feet across. She walked closer and brushed her hand across its surface. It looked like an altar, or at least some kind of ceremonial rock. She bent down to examine it and traced her hand over the faint outlines of animal figures in red and brown pigments.

She shivered and wondered how far she was below the ocean floor. The slope had been gradual so she hadn't realized the extent of her descent.

This part of the cave was dim but better lit than the previous chambers, even though it was deeper underground. She scanned the chamber to locate the light source and noticed a pinprick of light beyond the pool, probably fifty feet away. Was the illumination an opening onto Valdes Island in the opposite side of the tunnel, or a second exit on De Courcy Island?

De Courcy, she decided. She pressed the light on her watch. According to the illuminated dial, she had been in the cave about thirty minutes. Not long enough to walk the three-mile distance across the channel. Aside from several stops, she had also taken several twists and turns. It would take an hour to cover a three-mile distance at a brisk pace, and longer still with her limping gait.

It had been at least forty minutes since she saw Pete, and longer still since she separated from Jace and Raphael on the trail. She really ought to get back to the beach. But it wouldn't hurt to check out the other side of the pool. She'd kick herself later if she was right by the pool but didn't check it out. She allowed herself another five minutes. Then she would definitely turn back. At least that way she could describe the pool and tell the others what they had missed. When she returned with everyone else, she'd bring a flashlight.

She took one last look at the waterfall, eerily beautiful in the dim light. She turned to the source of light and headed to the narrow passageway. Had Brother XII followed this same path years earlier? Rumor had it that his jars of gold were hidden all over the island. Why not here? This was the perfect hiding place.

The light grew and then dimmed as she ventured further into the passageway. Within minutes it was completely dark and again she walked blindly through the tunnel with her hand on the moist cave wall. Moss and lichen tickled her palm. She slid her palm along the slick surface and tried not to think about what else besides water was under her hand.

"Ouch!" The cave floor dropped off beneath her. She fell into water and panicked as it encased her. The frigid water entered her lungs and nose as she sank underwater. She thrashed in the water, panicked that she couldn't tell the right way up.

One flip-flop popped off her foot and brushed her head as it passed above her. Her panic subsided when she realized it had floated to the surface. She pushed her body in the same direction and broke the water's surface. She gulped air as she righted herself. She coughed from the inhaled water and was surprised to find the water only waist deep. Still a problem, but wading was much better than swimming blindly.

She must have turned several times in an effort to right herself. Which direction had she come from? Her thoughts scrambled as she scanned the cave walls. She no longer saw the passageway, or any opening at all.

Everything looked the same in the dim light.

Her impromptu exploration may have been a fatal mistake.

Chapter 11

Victims panic, survivors survive. Kat silently repeated the mantra and willed herself to think calmly. She had read somewhere that many fire victims were only inches from safety when they died. They became disoriented and chose the wrong direction. She faced a similar situation, except that she had plenty of oxygen and wasn't in imminent danger.

She was lost, but she hadn't traveled any significant distance. She simply had to find the ledge and climb back up again. She had to reverse course methodically or risk getting herself even more lost.

She cursed under her breath. She had extricated herself from trouble minutes ago, only to put herself in a worse situation. No matter how many natural wonders she might see, this time she was heading back. Exploring a cave without a flashlight was a recipe for disaster.

No more solo explorations, she promised herself.

Just as soon as she got back on course.

She carried her flip-flops in her left hand and inched to the right. She counted a dozen steps and she was still in the water. She reversed course and counted fourteen steps when her thigh butted against a ledge. She smiled. It felt like the same ledge where she had slipped into the water.

She boosted herself up and considered that there could be more than one ledge. She'd better be certain she was headed in the right direction before going further.

She slipped back into the water and returned in the direction she had come. She counted fourteen steps. From there she counted an additional eight steps for a total of twenty-two steps before she came upon a similar ledge, only this time it was knee-level. She dropped a flip-flop on the ledge as a marker. Then she stepped up onto the ledge.

She reached a dead end less than twenty feet later. The passage's light source was an opening in the cave's roof. It was too small and far away to really see anything. That further alarmed her, since it meant she was much deeper underground than she had realized.

At least her questions were answered. As she turned, her knee protested with a sharp stab of pain. She reached down and found it was swollen. The sooner she reached the boat, the better, but it would be slow going. Jace's annoyance would have turned to worry by now.

She retraced her steps once more and returned to the ledge. She felt around for her flip-flop.

Nothing.

Just as she had feared. Because she hadn't walked in a straight line, she had arrived at a different spot on the ledge. The missing flip-flop was proof of that. Now she second-guessed all her earlier directions. If she was way off course, she'd never even know it. Even worse, she now had only one flip-flop.

She sighed and slipped back into the water. It rose to chest-level, much higher than it had been where she left the flip-flop. She inched along the ledge, feeling for her shoe. Her pulse quickened as she came up empty.

Survivors survive.

She suddenly smacked against a wall that blocked her way forward.

A wall that hadn't been there before.

She had taken a wrong turn, but where? Up until the waterfall, she had been careful to keep her hand along the wall, so she had to be headed back in the right direction.

That is, until she dropped off the ledge and had hurt her leg. That must be where she got turned around. In her excitement at finding the waterfall, she had forgotten to trace her steps along the cave wall. She realized in horror she was lost.

And alone. The family had obviously never entered the cave or she would have encountered them by now. Jace and the others would return to search for her, but would they venture this far into the cave? Would they even check the cave at all? As far as they knew, she hadn't gone near the cave. Then there was the wrong turn she'd made. They might never find her.

Her only hope was Pete. Once they realized she was missing, he'd tell them to check the cave. She brightened at the thought.

"Hello?" her voice echoed unanswered throughout the cavern.

But what if Pete didn't say anything? He didn't like her prying questions, and if he had something to hide, he might be worried about her uncovering it. She was safely out of the way. Surely Pete wouldn't be so cruel as to leave her trapped and alone in a cave.

Or would he?

What if he did? How on earth could she reach anyone? Her cell phone didn't work in the cave. Then it dawned on her.

Of course. While her cell phone wouldn't transmit a signal, it had a light. Why hadn't she thought of that before? Better late than never. She pulled it out of her pocket, thankful that she had thought to place it in a plastic bag for the short trip in the dinghy. She pulled it from the bag, pressed a button and her phone sprang to life. Seconds later the phone's flashlight illuminated a few feet around her.

The opening to the smaller cave was just three feet away. She had gotten turned around. She waded towards the entrance and boosted herself up onto the ledge. She knelt and grabbed her flip-flop. This time it took a bit longer to get back on her feet. Her knee was stiff and swollen, and so was her ankle. She swore as she stood. She limped towards the opening and walked through the tunnel.

Her hopes soared as she heard animal, or maybe bird noises. That meant she was close to an exit. Funny that she hadn't noticed the noise before.

The light was a lifesaver, but in some ways it was better in the dark. The illumination worsened her claustrophobia. For the first time, she clearly saw her surroundings. A breeze fluttered on her arm as something flew a few inches above her head. She grimaced as she realized it was a bat. It seemed to follow her path and landed in an alcove directly in front of her.

As she stared at the bat, she realized the entire shelf was moving. Hundreds of bats perched upside-down above her. She shuddered, wondering how she could have mistaken the sound for animals. The refreshing coolness of moments ago was suddenly suffocating. She willed herself to think calm sunny thoughts. In minutes she'd be out in the sunlight, or at least on the trail. At least that's what she told herself.

Relax.

Her trip inside had taken almost an hour, but her exit should be less than ten minutes.

Or maybe a bit longer, since it was increasingly hard to walk with her injured leg.

However long it took, she didn't care. She was back in familiar surroundings and she just needed to follow the path. Her spirits were buoyed as the waterfall came into view. She trudged past the pool and toward the opening to the next chamber as the familiar mist returned.

Soon she was in the outermost chamber. She just had to locate the rock outcropping with the notched rock to guide her around the corner. She had only felt the notch before, not seen it, so she traced her hand along the cave wall to locate it. She'd be outside and back on the trail within minutes. That was her last thought as she fell.

Chapter 12

Kat gasped as a spasm of pain shot through her leg.

She had tripped on the uneven ground and tumbled down off the path. She was so focused on finding the notched rock that she hadn't noticed the steep drop off beside the path. Her swollen knee and twisted ankle made it increasingly hard to walk and keep her balance. By favoring her good leg, she had gone over on her ankle and tripped as she stepped into a gaping hole.

That was the least of her worries, though. She was stuck between a rock and a hard place.

Literally.

Kat's fall had dislodged several rocks and her arm was pinned underneath some of them. She cursed under her breath as she considered the odds of getting hurt three times in less than an hour. Was she really that clumsy?

No, just plain stupid.

What had she been thinking, wearing flip-flops and hiking alone? But she hadn't started out alone.

She sighed and pulled out her phone to illuminate her surroundings. She was just a few feet away from the cave opening, so close she could almost taste the fresh air. The scent was probably just her mind playing tricks on her, but her cell phone's increased signal display was most definitely not her imagination. Against all odds, she had cell phone reception again. She punched in Jace's number and called him.

"Kat, where are you?" His voice cut in and out. "We've been looking all over for you."

"Stuck inside the cave." Pete knew she had gone to the cave. Surely he would have heard an uproar on the yacht as they tried to figure out where she was. Or maybe they hadn't even noticed her missing. But she really didn't want to think about that.

"How is that possible? The cave is only a few feet deep."

"No, it's bigger than that. I found a hidden opening. I stumbled across it almost by accident. But enough about that. You've got to get me out. I'm stuck."

"Stuck how?"

She briefly described her situation. "The details aren't important, and I don't want to waste my cell phone battery. I've fallen a few times. Maybe you could bring me a walking stick or something. And shoes."

There was a long pause at the other end. "Okay."

"Ask Pete about the cave. He's familiar with it."

"Who's Pete?"

"One of Raphael's crew. You must have seen him on the trail. He was there the same time as us."

"I didn't see anyone on the trail. There was a guy on the beach, though." Jace described him. "Now that you mention it,

Raphael seemed to know him. He talked to him for a few minutes before we went back to the ship."

"That's him. Kind of grizzly looking." She was surprised Jace hadn't noticed him aboard the yacht. But then again, Jace had sat at the bar, pretty much glued to Raphael's side, for most of the trip.

"He told Raphael you were heading back with him. That's why Raphael and I went back to the ship."

"That's ridiculous, Jace. Pete swam to the island." At least that was what Pete had told her.

"Why would he swim there when he could have come in the dinghy with us?"

"I have no idea, but that's beside the point. You don't even wonder if I'm okay, and now you take Raphael's word over mine?" Her face flushed as she tried to remain calm. "What if he was a criminal or something?"

"I guess I wasn't thinking right. Since Raphael knew him, I figured everything was okay." The first trace of doubt appeared in his voice.

"Raphael's from Italy, and we're visiting an island he's never been to before, and he knows some scruffy-looking beach bum?" If that wasn't proof of Raphael's inconsistent story, she didn't know what was.

"Don't be mad at me. You just confirmed he's one of the crew, so it all worked out in the end, right?"

"That's not the point, Jace." Arguing wouldn't get her out of the cave, but she needed to know what Pete's involvement was. "Did Pete tell you himself or was it relayed by Raphael?"

"Raphael," Jace admitted.

"Pete knew I was trying to catch up with you. Why would he lie?" Pete hadn't lied, but Raphael had. Jace wouldn't believe that though. He was so enamored with Raphael that he wouldn't believe anything negative about him. Raphael had lied to get rid of her. Anger welled upside her. "How was I supposed to get back to the yacht when you guys had the dinghy?"

"Pete said he'd take you back in his boat."

"Raphael told you that too, huh?"

Silence.

"Raphael knew there was only one dinghy." Pete almost certainly would have offered to help find her. Had Raphael quashed that too?

"Oh."

"That's all you can say?"

Jace sighed. "I'm sorry, okay. I just assumed that you were fine with Pete. With it being such a small island and all…"

"Just come get me out of this cave."

"I will. As soon as I find Raphael. I don't know where the dinghy is."

Her cell phone beeped its low battery warning. "My phone's dying. Just hurry." She would talk to Pete when she was back on board and get his side of the story, but she already knew what it was. "Get Pete to come with you. He's been inside the cave before."

"Don't worry," Jace said. "We'll get you out. I'm sure Raphael has lots of tools on the yacht."

"Just get here as fast as you can." Kat realized it was almost dinner time. Darkness wasn't far off, and rescue would be difficult once evening set in. The last thing she wanted was to spend the night in a damp, dark cave. Why was she constantly getting into these messes? Because her curiosity got the better of her, every time.

Her thoughts drifted back to Brother XII and his settlement. The settlers had bought into his dream without a second thought. More than a few of them had disappeared without a trace. She shivered at the thought and wondered if some rested within the cavern walls, lost like she was.

Brother XII's disciples had handed over their money, toiled on the land for nothing, only realizing too late that they had been swindled. Perhaps some had ventured into this very cave, looking to escape, or maybe in search of Brother XII's rumored treasure.

Of course Brother XII's treasure was really theirs, since it was amassed from the money they had surrendered when they joined the group. Perhaps they regretted handing over all their money to Brother XII and had come to get it back. They sought a way off the island, but once penniless, had no home to run to.

The lost souls in Brother XII's era had to find their own escape. No one searched for them or notified the authorities. They were forgotten people who ceased to exist in the outside world. When they surrendered to the Aquarian Foundation, they vanished through time.

She shuddered at the thought. She might have vanished in the cave, if not for the modern convenience of a cell phone.

She was jolted from her thoughts by a man's voice.

"Kat, can you hear me?" Raphael's voice came from the direction of the entrance. His voice was muffled, probably due to the cave acoustics or lack thereof.

"Over here. Straight in to the wall, then make a left. Where's Jace?"

"What? I can't hear you." His voice faded.

"Walk straight in to the back wall," Kat shouted. "Then follow the wall to the left." Why couldn't he hear her? While his voice was muffled, she could hear him just fine without him shouting.

Suddenly there was a deafening crash of rock, stone, and boulder.

The pale light vanished, replaced by blackness. The small opening was now completely closed off.

Something had blocked her exit.

Something, or someone.

Chapter 13

The boulder slammed against the small opening, cutting off Kat's only exit. The only voice she heard outside was Raphael's. In fact, she hadn't heard Jace at all.

"Jace? You there?" Why was Raphael doing the talking and not Jace?

Silence.

"Raphael, where's Jace?" She flashed back to Jace's comment about the dinghy. He said he couldn't find it. Yet Raphael was here. Had he returned to the island alone? "Who's with you, Raphael?"

No answer.

"Let me out!" Raphael obviously disliked her, but trapping her in a cave was tantamount to murder. Her heart raced as she wondered about Jace, Harry and Gia's whereabouts. Any one of them would drop everything to search for her. Jace knew she was trapped, so why wasn't he already here? Panic welled up inside her.

Maybe something had happened to them, too.

She was probably just being paranoid. But if that was the case, why didn't Raphael answer her? She was only certain about two things: she had recognized Raphael's voice outside the cave, and the rock that now blocked the exit hadn't moved there by itself. Raphael had trapped her in the cave instead of rescuing her.

That was crazy, unless Raphael had a secret much more sinister than defrauding Gia. While she was certain Raphael was swindling Gia out of her money, her friend wasn't exactly a millionaire. Raphael could easily cover his tracks and take the money and run. He didn't have to commit murder to get away with it.

There was something more, but she had only suspicions and no facts to explain his extreme behavior. What could possibly be enough to kill her?

Jace was very wrong about Raphael, but unless he came to his senses, he wouldn't assume Raphael had ulterior motives. And he would trust Raphael to rescue her. She flashed back to their phone conversation. Jace still didn't suspect anything wrong.

Footsteps crunched outside.

"What's happening?"

Kat's cry was met with silence. Her heart raced and she was suddenly claustrophobic. The cave seemed even darker and the air mustier.

Mind over matter.

Jace would get her out. He would be here in a flash.

If he could.

Her chest tightened as panic engulfed her. Had something happened to him, too? Whatever Raphael was hiding, he considered it worth the risk to trap her in the cave. He would leave her to die if he could.

Stop it.

Survivors survive.

A dozen slow breaths later, she came to one unmistakable conclusion. She wouldn't escape by passively waiting for a rescue. For starters, she needed to free her arm. She winced in pain as she wriggled her arm back and forth. After several minutes and rocking back and forth she finally worked it free. She sighed in relief at her close call. Now she had to get back on the path. She rolled the rocks off her stomach and sat up. She scrambled back up to level ground and limped to the cave opening.

She pushed against the rock, knowing even before she tried that it was futile. It didn't budge.

Defeated, she leaned against the rock. Her throat was parched with thirst. She hadn't even thought to bring a water bottle since they had planned only a very short hike. As if on cue, her stomach rumbled, hungry.

She had used up most of her cell phone battery with the flashlight. Would it work at all now that the cave was closed in?

It was all she had. She punched in Jace's number. Her spirits lifted as the call went through. She would be out of here in minutes, or at worst, an hour.

Her heart sank as her call went straight to Jace's voicemail. That worried her. Jace never turned his cell phone off.

Her battery indicator beeped, so she left a message for him. She spoke quickly and gave instructions on the rock's location blocking the hidden entrance and how to maneuver inside the cave. She was careful not to implicate Raphael just in case he had Jace's cell phone.

Uncle Harry was her last hope. She hoped she had enough battery juice to reach him. There was a good chance he hadn't even brought his cell phone with him though. Even when he had it in his pocket, he tended not to hear it. She entered his number and waited.

One, two, three rings, no answer.

Uncle Harry answered on the fourth ring. "Kat, where the heck are you? We've been waiting for you."

"I'm in a cave on the island."

"You're what? I can barely hear you. Maybe you should call back—"

"No—don't hang up. Listen carefully, Uncle Harry." She inched closer to the rock-covered opening in an attempt to increase her signal. "Find Pete and tell him I'm trapped in the cave."

"What cave? What's Pete got to do with anything?"

"It's not important right now. Just get him and come over here."

"But Raphael's got the dinghy…" Harry's voice faded, then cut off abruptly as her phone went dead.

She stared at her phone, deflated. At least she had made the call, and Uncle Harry knew she was in the cave. Small consolation, but help would arrive eventually. She could depend on her uncle for that. What she couldn't depend upon though, was his discretion. He would surely involve Raphael before Pete.

That was a problem. In the end it didn't matter, she decided. No matter how awkward, her uncle would persist in finding her. She would deal with Raphael once she was out.

She slid down against the cave wall into a sitting position and broke into a cold sweat. Very few people knew these caves existed, and from what Pete had told her, fewer still knew about the corridors and turns in this particular cave. With the rock blocking the opening, the entrance was invisible to anyone unfamiliar with the cave. She could die in here, slowly starving as the few cave visitors explored other corridors. She shivered and wrapped her arms around her knees

It also dawned on her that she, Uncle Harry, Jace and—as far as she knew—Gia, had told no one about their impromptu trip. Nobody knew of their whereabouts. Raphael could get rid of all of them. There wasn't a soul who knew where they were right now. It defied belief, but then so did blatantly trapping her in a cave.

If and when she was discovered, would she be just another artifact?

Chapter 14

Kat jolted awake. Someone or something else was in the cave. She held her breath and listened. The scratching noise was close, just a few feet away near the entrance. She shuddered and remembered the bats. She was hardly the only living creature in the cave.

She held her breath and listened to see how close it was. It wasn't an animal after all. Her hopes soared as metal clanged against rock. Somebody was outside.

"Help me!" She jumped to her feet and winced in pain. In her exhilaration she forgot her swollen ankle and injured knee. She stumbled backwards. "I'm trapped inside the cave."

No answer.

She must have dozed off. She had drained her watch battery and it was now too dark to see the dial unaided. Her cell phone battery was dead too, so she had no idea how much time had passed. It couldn't be that long. She was hungry, but not ravenously so. Her last meal had been lunch on the ship.

"In here!"

Silence.

Momentary elation was replaced by disappointment. Her mind was playing tricks on her. There was no one else here, as much as she wished otherwise. Maybe she had dreamt the whole thing.

"Anyone out there?"

Silence.

It was much darker inside the cave now that the rock blocked the entrance. It was also closer to nightfall.

The scratching sounded again.

Her hopes faded. An animal was probably burrowing or digging outside. No chance of help there.

But the sound increased, and once again she heard metal against rock. Unless there were tool- wielding animals inside the cave, metal was a good sign.

Better than good. It was music to her ears. Like a symphony.

She focused on the sound and tried to identify it.

"You there?" Jace's voice was clear. He couldn't be more than ten feet away.

"Yes! Get me out of here, Jace." She'd better not have dreamt his voice. "Can you hear me okay?"

"Yeah. Are you all right?"

"Pretty much." Relief flooded over her. She would finally be freed.

"Thank goodness!" Uncle Harry chimed in. "We'll get you out, Kat. Hang tight."

She had never felt so lucky in her life. "It's so good to hear your voices. I'm so glad you found me. What time is it?"

"Just after seven o'clock. We got worried when you didn't return," Jace said. By the sound of his voice, he was doing something physical. That explained the shovel sounds.

"But I was with you and Raphael. Why did you leave without me?" She had no idea if Raphael was outside with them, but she wanted an answer now. She couldn't wait any longer.

"You told us to."

"I did not," Kat said.

"Sure you did. You told Raphael you'd catch a ride back with Pete. I even double checked."

"I never said any such thing." Her word against Raphael's, but shouldn't her word count more? "I never even spoke to Raphael."

"He obviously misunderstood." Jace grunted. "This rock is wedged in here pretty tight. I don't have the right tools."

"A pry bar would work," Uncle Harry said. "There's no tools like that on the yacht, though."

Kat's heart sank. She had expected to be rescued in minutes, but things didn't sound very promising.

"I meant to say that Pete relayed your message to Raphael. So that's why we left."

"Did you check with Pete on that?"

"No, I guess I should have." Jace's words came in short bursts as he shoveled. "Raphael obviously got it wrong. But you're partially to blame for going off on your own like that. We couldn't figure out where you were."

Or notice I was gone, Kat thought. Her elation was eclipsed by anger as she remembered how Jace had simply forgotten she was there.

"That's when we realized you were still here," Uncle Harry said. "Pete said you didn't return with him. He seems a bit forgetful if you ask me."

Her impression of Pete was entirely different than her uncle's. But now wasn't the time or place to ask more. She'd wait until she was safely back on the yacht. Of course, whether she was safe onboard was another story altogether. "How long till I'm out?"

"Depends," said Jace. "We've got to improvise, since all we've got are shovels. And not very sturdy ones at that. But our plan is slowly working."

"We're doing what the ancient Egyptians did, and digging the dirt and sand out from under the rock," Uncle Harry said. "We're hoping the rock will just roll forward."

"That's clever." She vaguely remembered a documentary she had watched with Jace. While it made sense, it also sounded dangerous. One wrong move and that rock could roll right on top of them. "Give me some warning before the rock rolls."

"Oh, that won't be for a while yet," Uncle Harry said.

She only heard one shovel and suspected Jace was doing most of the digging.

"What I can't figure out is how you got stuck behind this thing in the first place. It's huge." Jace sounded breathless.

"It wasn't there when I went in." As a matter of fact, Kat couldn't remember any boulders nearby. She hadn't been looking for them, though. She had been focused on whatever treasures might lay ahead of her. How had Raphael maneuvered it in front of the cave by himself? "How long do you think it will take?"

"Probably another twenty minutes if things go as planned," Jace said.

"Whoa!" Uncle Harry cried.

The rock shifted and a thin sliver of light shone above her. She had never been so happy to see the sky. The triangular-shaped opening was largest on the side farthest from her. Judging by the angle, the rock rested on uneven ground.

"That was a close one, Jace," Uncle Harry said. "We better watch out."

"Right," Jace said. "Harry, go find some long pieces of wood. We'll wedge them under the rock as we dig, then pull them out when we're ready. The rock should just roll right out with the downward momentum."

"Got it," Uncle Harry said.

Jace shoveled while Harry dragged logs and wood into place. Judging from all the grunts and curses, it was heavy, sweaty work. Kat wished she could help but instead listened guiltily.

After what seemed like an eternity they were finally ready. Which was a good thing, since the tiny sliver of sky above the rock had changed into a deep indigo blue. Soon it would be dark, so their plan had better work the first time.

"Let's do this," Jace said. "Kat, stand back just in case something else gets triggered. Harry, stand at the other side. Pull the first logs out when I say go. I'll do the same on this side."

"Gotcha."

"Now," Jace shouted. The rock lurched forward and exposed a larger opening. But the sides of the rock were still firmly wedged against the cave wall.

"Kat, can you climb up and over the top?" Jace asked.

"I don't think so. There aren't any footholds. I don't know how to boost myself up." Kat's heart sank. So close and yet so far. She had hoped to be out before nightfall, but things didn't look promising. In the meantime Raphael was probably robbing Gia blind and getting her to invest even more.

"I've got an idea. What if we had a rope?"

"That might work." She had tried indoor rock climbing once. She could probably manage. She had a glimmer of hope that she might be able to sleep in a bed tonight.

"Okay. Now we just need a rope." He was silent for a moment. "Harry, can you take the dinghy and get back to the ship? There's got to be rope on board."

"We don't have time for that, Jace." Raphael would purposely delay them. After all, he had intentionally trapped her in the first place. "Are you guys wearing belts?"

"Yep," Uncle Harry said.

"Yes, why?" Jace asked.

"One belt isn't long enough, but two might be."

"Worth a try. But are they strong enough to hold together?"

"Only one way to find out," Kat said. Would it work? All she could do was hope.

A leather belt slid down the rock. She reached up and grabbed it. She pulled and felt tension as Jace held the other end. She leaned back and stepped on the rock but couldn't pull herself up. The end of the belt was still too high above her head, and she didn't have the upper body strength to boost herself.

The belts had to be longer, or else she had to be higher. She looked for a rock small enough to move. She needed to stand on something a foot or so high. That would elevate her enough to pull herself up the rock.

But all the rocks around her were small. She gathered what she could and stacked them in a makeshift platform. She tested the stability with one foot. It was precarious even without her injuries, but it held. It was also her only option.

Here she was again in her flip-flops, another accident waiting to happen. She cursed under her breath. There was no other way, she thought as she stepped up with her other foot.

"Okay, I'm ready." Kat pulled on the belts until she felt the tension on the opposite end.

"Okay. Got it, Harry?" Jace asked.

"Yup. Go for it, Kat," Uncle Harry said.

"All right, here I come." She visualized her one and only rock-climbing experience at the indoor climbing center. She put one foot against the rock and leaned back about forty-five degrees. The belts held. She took a deep breath and stepped off the rock mound with her other foot. She focused on placing one foot in front of the other.

"So far, so good." Jace shouted. "Keep going."

She was within inches of the opening, but her muscles burned.

Kat didn't know whether the men held the belts or if they had tied them onto something else instead. She broke into a sweat. If it was this hard, she was probably doing it wrong. Her sweaty palms slid on the leather and her skin burned as she struggled to hang on.

She tightened her palm around the leather but it was no use. It slipped from her grip and she fell backwards, landing on the ground with the rock pile in the small of her back. She cried out in pain.

"What happened?" Jace asked.

"I lost my grip." Kat rolled onto her side and winced as spasms shot through her back, knee and ankle. "Give me a minute, then I'll try again."

"Just holler when you're ready," Harry said.

Pain or no pain, she was getting the hell out of this cave.

Ten minutes later, she reached the top of the rock. She paused and inhaled air deep into her lungs. The fresh air intoxicated her as she scrambled across the top. She smiled down at Jace and Harry who stood about ten feet below.

"You're sure a sight for sore eyes," Harry said.

"You guys too." She smiled and swiveled her legs over the edge. She almost jumped before she remembered her knee and ankle.

"What's wrong?" Harry asked.

"Nothing," she replied. Everything was wrong, but there wasn't much she could do about it. At least not yet. She braced herself and jumped. She cried out as she hit the ground on her side. She rolled over onto her butt and held up her hand for assistance.

Jace pulled her up. "I'm never letting you out of my sight again."

She could live with that.

Chapter 15

Kat sat on the bed, her back propped up against the headboard. Her leg was elevated with ice packs placed strategically around her swollen knee and twisted ankle. By the time they had returned to the yacht, her leg had morphed into one gigantic, swollen blob. She was exhausted from both her near-death cave experience and the hour-long limp back to the dinghy.

"You look like a casualty of war." Jace sat at the desk and typed on his keyboard. "How do you always manage to find trouble? We just went for a short walk in the woods."

More like trouble had found her. How could she broach the subject of Raphael's deception without sounding like a lunatic? Jace already figured she had it in for the guy. She needed Pete's confirmation of her version of events, but she wouldn't get any proof sitting in bed.

She swung her legs over the side of the bed and winced as she stood. She didn't even know where to find Pete onboard. Hopefully her search wouldn't involve a lot of walking.

Jace glanced up from his laptop screen. "You're not going anywhere. Tell me what you want and I'll get it for you."

She shook her head. "I just wanted to test out my leg, see how it's doing."

"We've been back for less than an hour." Jace shook his head. "That's not enough time to make any difference at all. It's going to swell more if you don't elevate it. What do you need?"

"Some fresh air. I'll prop my leg up once I'm outside."

"No you won't."

"Sure I will, I promise." She demonstrated what she hoped was a normal-looking walk. "It'll stiffen up if I don't move a little bit."

Jace raised his brows and shook his head. "I can't help you if you won't help yourself."

"Walking is good for me." She couldn't exactly ask him to go get Pete.

"You're not going to listen to me, are you?" He walked over and placed her arm over his shoulder. "You shouldn't be walking at all, let alone without crutches. I doubt that there are any crutches on board. Can't your walk wait till tomorrow?"

Her mind raced to find an excuse. "I need some air. I'm feeling a bit seasick."

"That's odd. We aren't even moving." Jace was doubtful.

"I still feel claustrophobic from the cave." She slipped on her flip-flops. "Luxurious or not, this room is still pretty small."

"Wait a sec, I'll grab your ice." Jace retrieved her icepack from the bed and followed her to the door.

He was right about one thing. She couldn't walk well enough to track down Pete. But if she sat on deck there was a small possibility he might walk by. The odds were equally good that she would see Raphael instead. She shivered at the thought. She'd take her chances.

She limped down the passageway and through the galley. Her swollen knee throbbed as she ascended the stairs to the deck. As she shifted her weight to the railing for support, she stifled a moan. She couldn't let Jace see how much it hurt, or he'd insist she return to bed.

Jace passed her and pulled the door open. A stiff breeze blew in. Refreshing, she thought as she exited outside.

Jace walked ahead of her and quickly pulled out a chaise lounge and arranged her ice packs. "Anything else you need from below deck?"

That was the opportunity she had been looking for. "Uh, maybe a book to read?"

"Tell me where your book is and I'll get it."

"I already finished the book I brought, but there must be other books onboard. Maybe in the living room? Just get me a good mystery or something." That would take him a few minutes, enough time to see if Pete was anywhere nearby.

Jace frowned. "I'm sure Raphael has books, but probably not your taste. You might not like what I pick out."

"I'll take that chance." She felt guilty for sending Jace on a made-up errand, but it bought her some time. Maybe she could just walk around the corner and see if Pete was around. She really needed her facts straight before making any accusations.

"All right." He disappeared below deck and Kat considered her strategy. She had ten minutes at best, so where to look first? She decided on the bridge. Even if Pete wasn't there, another crew member would likely know where to find him.

That turned out to be a good decision.

Pete was inside, seated at the controls with another crew member. She saw only the other man's back, but it was enough to know that he been chosen from a similar labor pool as Pete. He looked like a wharf rat who worked odd jobs for food, shelter, and off-the-record cash. Raphael's rag-tag crew appeared very temporary. They were the worst-looking bunch of professional mariners she had ever laid eyes on.

Pete stopped mid-sentence and scrutinized her. "Looks like you had an accident."

"You could call it that. Can I talk to you in private?"

He nodded at the other man who rose and exited.

A little too eagerly, Kat thought. There was one thing Raphael's crew members excelled at: keeping a low profile.

"I fell. But that's not why I'm here. Why did you tell Raphael I went back to the ship with you?"

"I never said that." He stumbled slightly as he stood up. "What are you talking about?"

"You let him and Jace leave me on the island. Someone trapped me in that cave."

"So you found the cave." He smiled, exposing yellowed teeth.

He reeked of alcohol. Kat's feigned nausea quickly turned real. "That's what I need to talk to you about."

Pete shouted something to his colleague who suddenly reappeared in the wheelhouse.

"Back in five," he said to his colleague before he turned to Kat. ""Let's go on deck."

She followed him, noting that his drunken gait wasn't much better than her limp. She had no trouble keeping up with him.

She thought the crew should at least be sober while on duty, even if they were anchored.

They headed to the main deck. Pete motioned around the corner to a small alcove Kat hadn't noticed before. He pulled out a grimy-looking chair and motioned for her to sit down.

He sat opposite her on a stool. "If you plan on stirring up trouble, I don't want no part in it."

Drunk Pete wasn't nearly as friendly as the sober version. "I'm not stirring up anything, but someone trapped me in that cave. I think it was Raphael."

"That's between you and him." He swayed slightly as he stood. "None of my business."

Kat stood and blocked his exit. "Raphael said you told him that I was staying on the island with you."

"That's a lie. I never said that." He crossed his arms as his face reddened. "We barely talked. He just told me to get back on board."

"How exactly did you get to the island? I didn't see another dinghy."

He paused for a moment. "Same way I got here. I swam."

"You swam?" She raised her brows. "Why didn't you just come with us?"

"Maybe I like to get my exercise." He shrugged. "I've gotta go."

"Not so fast. Why would Raphael lie? He knew you didn't have a boat." There was only one dinghy. Jace obviously hadn't overheard the conversation or he would have questioned it. Aside from her lack of swimming apparel, she was a lousy swimmer. In fact, she could barely float.

"Beats me. Why don't you ask him? You know him better than I do."

"No I don't. I just met him today."

"Oh." Pete suddenly seemed uncertain and his expression softened slightly. "Well, I haven't known him much longer than you, and I need this job. Can't help you." He turned sideways to brush past her.

"That leaves me with no other choice then." Kat shifted on her feet and winced as her weight transferred to her sore leg. Her movement stopped Pete his tracks.

He stepped back a few feet and frowned. "No other choice about what?"

"I'll have to call the police." Kat got the feeling Pete didn't want the police around, so she bluffed. He was definitely hiding something, and she wanted to know what it was. Knowledge of whatever arrangement Pete and Raphael had was important, since it gave her an idea of what Raphael had planned. She had no idea if there was a police detachment nearby, but their cell phones worked.

"Call them about what, exactly?"

"That someone purposely trapped me in a cave and tried to kill me. There were three men on the island. Any one of them could have done it. I'll let the police figure that part out." Of course Jace hadn't done it, but no point in confusing the issue. No reason to mention the family, either. While she knew Raphael had trapped her, Pete didn't. She decided to let him stew a little. It was the only way to get information out of him.

Pete slowly shook his head. "Bad idea."

"You think it's better to stay onboard with someone who's trying to kill me?"

"I never said that. You'll just make things worse."

Kat threw her hands up in the air. "Worse how, exactly?"

"Just don't do it."

She pulled out her phone. "Unless you tell me why I shouldn't…"

"Okay, fine. I'll tell you." He paused before continuing. "This here's an American boat. We came up from Friday Harbor, but we never went through Canada Customs."

Friday Harbor was a small port in the San Juan Islands, north of Seattle. "You snuck across the border?"

"It's not the huge deal you're making it out to be, but yeah, we did. We should have cleared customs in Vancouver, but since we didn't, we're here illegally."

"It's not your fault." She pressed some numbers on her phone and held it up to her face. "It's connecting."

Pete grabbed her phone and chucked it across the deck. "I only work here, I don't make the decisions. Raphael does. But I'm on the ship, so I'll get in trouble too."

"No you won't. Like you said, it wasn't your decision." Pete had reason to avoid the police, though she got the impression it was unrelated to Raphael. Maybe an outstanding warrant or something, but her gut told her he wasn't the problem.

She turned, intending to retrieve her phone.

Pete followed her gaze. "I'll get it for you." He walked over and picked it up. "Sorry, I shouldn't have done that. Just don't call the police. We'll be gone in a few days and it won't matter anymore." He handed her phone back.

Exactly the information she was looking for. "Where exactly are you going?"

He shrugged. "Nowhere that you need to know about."

"Why not sell it here?"

"Sell what?"

"The yacht."

Silence.

"*The Financier* isn't really Raphael's boat, is it?" It was a hunch, given that Raphael didn't seem very interested in cruising.

Pete shrugged, but his forehead glistened with a thin sheen of sweat. "Of course it's his. Raphael was already on the boat when I got on in Friday Harbor. He hired me and the other guys to crew."

"You don't think it's odd that he didn't already have a crew?"

"He said he'd been away for a few months and let his crew go. We were supposed to sail to Vancouver to meet them."

"What happened?"

"The crew never showed. Raphael said there was a mix up in dates or something, and that we'd trade off in Costa Rica instead. We were supposed to leave today, but then this detour trip came up, with you and your friends."

"What happens in Costa Rica?" She scratched her forehead. "Let me guess. You'll leave the boat there." A yacht this size was hard to disguise in these parts. But no one would ask questions in Central America. *The Financier* would just be another one of the many foreign yachts that called at Costa Rican ports along the coast. The yacht could be transformed completely at a maritime chop shop and sold there.

Pete shrugged. "He doesn't tell me, and I don't ask."

"How long are you staying there?" There was more to Costa Rica than sandy beaches and a laid back lifestyle. Canada had no extradition treaty with Costa Rica. Anyone hiding there was safe from Canadian authorities.

Now Kat was more certain than ever of Raphael's deception. But it was a lot of effort just for Gia's money. He had something else in play. Whoever he was, he most certainly wasn't an Italian billionaire. Once he reached Costa Rican shores, he would disappear forever.

"How will you get back here?"

Pete didn't answer.

"You're never coming back, are you?" Whatever skeletons hid in Pete's closet, he wasn't keen on discussing them.

"Gotta get back to work." Pete shook his head and waved his hand in dismissal. Then he disappeared around the corner without another word.

Chapter 16

Kat returned to her chaise lounge to find Jace already there. He sat on the adjacent chair with a handful of books. He held up an Agatha Christie novel as she approached and looked displeased with her vanishing act.

She couldn't picture Raphael reading Agatha Christie, though she had no idea what kind of books he liked, or if he even read at all.

Jace shook his head. "I shouldn't have left you alone. Why are you walking around? The swelling won't go down unless you keep your leg elevated."

"You're right." At least he hadn't asked where she'd gone. She wouldn't dare accuse Raphael of the cave entrapment without solid proof for Jace. Raphael was a cunning and charismatic manipulator and he'd just twist her words around.

Jace's professional skepticism as a journalist had been replaced by admiration to the extent that he'd find her claim outrageous without proof. Instead of questioning Raphael's every statement, he had been duped by his lies. Yet with

Raphael's impending departure, she had to expose him before it was too late. She didn't even know where to start.

"It could have been much worse. You're very lucky to escape. Never explore a cave by yourself like that. No one even knew you were in there."

Not true, since Raphael knew her whereabouts. Not only had he known she was inside the cave, he had prevented her escape.

"I know, stupid mistake." Once Jace and Harry removed the rock from the cave entrance, they had spent a few minutes exploring the outer cave by flashlight. Unbeknownst to her, Kat had stood less than fifteen feet from a vertical shaft that plunged a hundred feet or more down. She shivered just thinking about it.

"Next time, tell me where you're going." Careless missteps bothered Jace since they were easily preventable. As a search and rescue volunteer, he had witnessed many tragedies that resulted from poor planning. It irked him that she had gone off on her own in unfamiliar territory.

"I will, promise." Too bad Jace couldn't see through Raphael's veil of charisma. She needed proof of his character and ulterior motives. She couldn't prove Raphael had trapped her in the cave. It was her word against Raphael's.

She had more immediate worries based on what Pete had just told her. If Raphael had originally planned to leave for Costa Rica today, why had he delayed things? He already had Gia's money. Had he found another money-making opportunity? And why had he offered to bring them to De Courcy in the first place?

Jace read her mind. "You know, Raphael is a smart guy. He's doing us a huge favor by allowing us in on his investment opportunity. You sure you won't change your mind?"

"Friends and money don't mix well, Jace." Enemies and money were even worse.

"This is different. It's a once in a lifetime opportunity that might never happen again. If we pass it up, we'll miss the next big thing."

"If it's so great, we'll still be able to invest tomorrow. The company will need more money to expand."

Jace looked doubtful. "Maybe, maybe not. We should take a closer look. Gia's smart and she's invested."

"No, Jace." Clearly Raphael was a con artist and she needed all her focus on helping Gia. "He can't even show us any product, let alone sales and financial information."

"It was good enough for Gia to invest. She knows what she's doing."

"From the sounds of it, Gia invested without looking at all those things." Gia was blinded by love. Jace was blinded by the promise of riches.

Jace sighed. "By the time you analyze it all to death, we'll miss out on the opportunity."

"Maybe. But he's short on details about how his product actually works. I can't invest in something I don't understand."

"You can ask him at dinner." Jace held out his hand. "Let's go."

"You mean you guys haven't already eaten?"

"Of course not. Everyone was looking for you. C'mon. I'm starving." Jace was disappointed.

"My stomach's a bit queasy." Her appetite had been replaced by a sick feeling in her gut. It scared her that Gia was in love with a man who thought nothing of leaving someone to die in a cave. What did he have in store for Gia? She couldn't face Raphael without a plan of attack. "My leg is still sore too."

Jace gave her an I told you so look. "I'll bring you back a snack."

He headed inside before she could answer.

Great. Jace was mad at her again. So was everyone on board, and she had no proof to convince them otherwise. She had her work cut out for her if she was to expose Raphael's true motives. Based on Pete's comments, Raphael was about to take the money and run. He was about to put his plans into motion, and she had to stop him before it was too late.

Chapter 17

Kat sat propped up on her stateroom bed, laptop open beside her. Thankfully she was able to get an Internet connection, but her online search for both Raphael and *The Financier* came up empty. A yacht like this probably showed up somewhere online, either in a photograph or on a manufacturer's website. Her conversation with Pete had given her an idea.

Only a handful of companies built large luxury yachts like Raphael's, and she soon had a list of a half dozen companies. The yachts were mostly hand built, and they often took a year or more to complete. If she found the shipbuilder, she might be able to trace the yacht's ownership. One way or another, she'd expose Raphael as a fraud.

Who would illegally enter Canada and risk having their multi-million dollar yacht seized? Not even a billionaire would do that. But a thief would.

She scanned the list and clicked on the first name, Prima Yachts.

Nothing.

Her hopes already dashed, she checked the second entry on the list. Majestic Yachts, a company based in Seattle, Washington, had a listing of new and pre-owned yachts for sale. She smiled as she imagined billionaires trading in their older yachts for newer models, sort of like she did with her car. They probably didn't wait a dozen years, though.

A stroke of luck. A ship identical to *The Financier* was listed, except it had a different name. Catalyst was four years old, with an asking price of $6.9 million US dollars.

The 150-foot yacht had four double cabins and accommodations for six crew. There were just four crew on board including Pete, so they probably had their hands full operating a ship meant for a larger crew. Raphael appeared uninvolved in the yacht's operation, and she hadn't seen a cook or other staff on board.

A skeleton staff might be fine for short trips in sheltered waters, but no one would skimp on crew labor and risk a seven-million-dollar shipwreck.

She scrolled through the Catalyst photographs, squinting to make out the details. The ship appeared identical to *The Financier*, right down the color schemes and furniture. It struck her as odd that a custom-built ship had an identical twin.

She put the yacht search on hold for the moment and considered what she knew about Raphael.

The fact that she had turned up nothing on Raphael convinced her he was a fake. But she had no concrete proof to show the others, especially Gia. Gia would never believe that the man she loved—and had invested with—had also duped her.

Maybe Jace was right. Her line of work made her naturally suspicious of people. Rightly or wrongly, she was interfering in Gia's life. What would Gia say if she knew Kat was searching Raphael's background to find reasons for Gia to dump him? Gia would tell her to mind her own business.

But keeping her worries to herself only hurt Gia in the end. Sometimes friends knew best.

Despite her misgivings, her online search had revealed nothing at all about Raphael. She should have found at least a smattering of public information on someone who claimed to be a billionaire. Yet there was nothing about him or his company. That in itself was a red flag.

She had scrolled through all the beauty supply trade journals and company websites and came up empty. Then there was his yacht. Pete hadn't confirmed *The Financier* was stolen, but he hadn't denied it either. *The Financier* was either Catalyst's very unlikely identical twin, or it was the Catalyst in disguise.

Another odd thing about Raphael was the amount of leisure time he enjoyed. Kat had met plenty of billionaires and millionaires in her prior life as a finance consultant. She had yet to find a single tycoon who didn't plan their schedule weeks in advance down to the nearest millisecond. Their leisure time was equally parsed. They rarely had time for spontaneous trips like Raphael's spur-of-the-moment De Courcy Island excursion. Raphael was either unique or not who he pretended to be.

Whoever Raphael really was, he was very good at covering his tracks. And he was about to disappear for good.

She shut her laptop off. Raphael was the last person she wanted to see, but she had to go upstairs. It was a mistake to stay in the stateroom away from the others. Aside from Raphael himself, Gia was her only source of information to get at the heart of Raphael's scheme. She needed to spend every waking moment around the couple to both expose his lies and prevent Gia from investing more.

She checked her watch. Jace had only been gone twenty minutes, so it wasn't too late for dinner. She slipped into her shoes. She could play nice for an hour or two.

Kat exited the cabin and noticed the master stateroom door ajar. Gia must have returned to freshen up. Now was as good a time as any to talk to Gia privately and determine exactly how much Raphael had shared with her about his past.

She knocked softly.

No response.

"Gia?"

She peered through the door crack and saw no movement. Should she go in?

She debated knocking louder but didn't want anyone else to hear.

This might be her only opportunity to get Gia alone, she decided. She inched the door open and stepped inside.

The stateroom was empty. She turned to leave but hesitated. She hadn't purposely trespassed, and she had a perfect opportunity for a quick look around. She might find a clue to unmask Raphael's motives.

What if she ran into Raphael? How on earth would she explain her reason for being here?

She would use the excuse that Gia had asked her to grab something.

She scanned the room again and headed for the bathroom, which was also vacant. The stateroom was twice the size of hers, and even more luxurious. Gia's presence was everywhere, from the overflowing closet to the perfume and jewelry scattered about the dresser. She had pretty much moved in with Raphael.

Kat limped towards the dresser and almost tripped over a woman's wallet on the floor. She bent to pick it up, thinking it had fallen from Gia's purse. She was about to place it on the dresser when she noticed the initials MB embossed on the worn black leather. A lot of designer wallets and purses had monograms, but this wallet was decidedly not designer ware. Aside from being old, the wallet was basic and utilitarian, the polar opposite of Gia's glittery fashion taste. If it wasn't Gia's wallet, whose was it?

One way to find out. Her heart pounded as she opened the wallet. She had absolutely no reason to be in Raphael and Gia's stateroom, much less to be rifling through a stranger's wallet.

She pulled out a driver's license. It belonged to a woman named Anne Bukowski. According to her identification, she was 30 years old and lived in Vancouver. Perhaps Gia or Raphael had found the wallet and planned to return it.

Or perhaps Raphael had another girlfriend. She was betting on the second.

"What are you doing in here?" Raphael stood in the doorway.

Startled, Kat shoved the wallet in her back pocket. "Uh, just looking for Gia. I was supposed to meet her here."

"She's upstairs, like everyone else." Raphael swept his arm in an exit motion. "After you."

"Thanks." She felt her face flush, uncertain if he had seen her pocket the wallet. If he had, he surely would have said something.

The bigger question was, what was another woman's wallet doing in Raphael's room?

There were any number of innocent explanations. Maybe he had found it, or perhaps it was left behind by a former guest. The more likely answer was that Anne was either a current or ex-girlfriend. She doubted that Gia had seen the wallet because she would have flipped out, and Kat would have heard of it.

Gia would never know, now that Kat had removed the wallet from the stateroom. She would return it later. It would be best if Gia found it herself and questioned Raphael directly. It was none of her business, so she'd stay out of it.

Whatever Raphael's explanation, it probably wouldn't fly with Gia. Gia might be temporarily heartbroken, but she would also break up with Raphael and maybe even get her money back. That might actually be a good thing. Kat didn't hold out much hope for the latter, though.

She ascended the stairs, deep in thought. She was no longer hungry, and with the wallet discovery, wanted only to return to the privacy of her stateroom. Who was Anne Bukowski, and how did she figure into Raphael's scheme?

Chapter 18

Kat brushed past Raphael and headed upstairs, one painful step at a time. Raphael followed close behind. As she limped upstairs, the wallet inched upwards in her back pocket. She reached behind and shoved it further down. If Raphael noticed, he didn't say anything.

How long had he watched her from the doorway? Her pulse quickened as she remembered the security cameras. He could have seen her enter the stateroom on CCTV. If he had, though, he would have confronted her about it That didn't mean he couldn't review footage later, though. She could still be discovered.

What was done was done, and there wasn't much she could do about it. She would be more careful next time.

Finally she and her swollen leg reached the main deck and she headed into the galley. Or rather, the separate dining room just off of the galley, where the others were already seated.

"About time." Harry waved and stood. He pulled out a chair, which Kat gratefully accepted. Jace sat to her right and Harry on her left, with Raphael and Gia seated opposite them.

"Looks like you got your appetite back," Harry grinned. "Less for me."

"There's plenty for everyone," Gia said. "Glad you're feeling better, Kat."

Kat smiled back. Gia appeared to have forgiven her, at least for now. She reached behind her and pushed the fat wallet back in her pants pocket. Her back pocket was too shallow to hide the wallet's bulge while sitting. She could barely wait to get back to her stateroom to investigate its contents.

"I'm dying to hear about your adventure," Gia said. "Find any gold in the cave?"

"No, but I found an interesting passageway." She mentioned Pete's claims of aboriginal artifacts. "According to legend, there's a tunnel from De Courcy Island to Valdes Island. It goes a few hundred feet underground. Under the sea, as a matter of fact. I think I was in it."

"Cool!" Harry almost knocked his glass over in his excitement. "Did you come out the other side?"

She shook her head. "I didn't go far enough into the passage. It was dark and I hadn't brought a flashlight. Or, as it turns out, the right shoes."

"Maybe the gold is there," Jace said. "Let's go back tomorrow and explore."

Gia turned to Raphael, who was uncharacteristically silent. "Is Kat the only one that saw anything?"

"I guess Jace and I missed it." He stood and walked into the galley. He opened the refrigerator and grabbed a bottle of salad dressing. He brought it to the table. "Our bad luck."

Gia frowned. She turned to Kat. "Tell us about the legend."

She repeated what Pete had told her. "The Coast Salish and other tribes used the tunnel as a rite of passage for young men. They carried their wooden staffs along the three-mile tunnel under the ocean and deposited them at the other end of the tunnel as proof of their journey."

"You must have been in the very same tunnel!" Gia exclaimed. "Did you see any artifacts?"

"I'm not sure," Kat wasn't keen on describing the stone altar—if that's what it was. If it was a sacred place she didn't want to disturb the solitude by bringing others there. She hadn't seen any evidence of its use; it was more just a feeling she'd had as she stood in front of it.

"I didn't see any wooden staffs or masks. But I did see a waterfall." She described it and the pool. "It was quite beautiful. It was so dark though, so I couldn't really see much. I saw some graffiti, too, so I can't be the only one that knows about the cave."

"How far did you go into the tunnel?" Raphael asked.

"Probably about a mile or so," Kat said. "I'd like to go back. This time with a flashlight. I think I was halfway to Valdes Island, but it's impossible to know. I never made it to the other side."

Raphael scoffed. "That's just an old legend, like Brother XII and the gold. It's probably just a tunnel that goes nowhere. There are plenty of them around."

Kat's anger rose, but then she realized Raphael had been caught in a lie. "I didn't know you'd been to the island before."

"Huh?"

"You know the tunnels and caves."

"Just from what Pete told me." He laughed nervously. "Probably just a bunch of made-up stories."

"I'd still like to see the cave," Jace said. "I don't know how we missed it. Maybe we can go early tomorrow and explore."

Harry held up his arm. "Count me in this time. You should skip it, Kat. Rest your leg instead."

"It feels better already. A good night's sleep and I'll be just like new." In truth it felt horrible, but she wasn't admitting that in front of Raphael.

"I'd like to see for myself, too. And talk to Pete," Jace turned to Raphael. "Can he join us? He seems to know a lot about the island."

Raphael shrugged. "Probably. But let's decide tomorrow."

Jace nodded. "It would make a great addition to my story. This is turning into a fantastic trip."

Raphael nodded and raised his wine glass. "I'd like to propose a toast. To Gia, the love of my life."

Gia blushed. "Should we tell them the news, Raphael?"

Kat turned to Gia. "What news?"

"If you're ready, bellissima," Raphael placed his hand on top of Gia's.

Kat braced herself. Things could get much worse if Gia had invested even more.

"We're getting married." Gia giggled. "Isn't that wonderful?"

"You're what?" Kat gasped. Even if her instincts were wrong about Raphael—which they weren't—Gia hardly knew him and was so blinded by love that she couldn't see through his lies.

"You heard right. We're tying the knot." Gia lifted her left hand, which was adorned with a mega-carat diamond solitaire. It looked gigantic on her chubby little hand.

"That's fantastic," Jace exclaimed. "We're so happy for you." He nudged Kat. "Aren't we, Kat?"

Bile rose in Kat's throat. "That's exciting news. Have you set a date?"

"No, but the sooner the better." Raphael squeezed Gia's hand. "I can't let her get away."

Kat's pulse quickened. The only thing Raphael didn't want to lose was Gia's money.

"Oh Raphael, don't be silly. I'm not going anywhere." Gia caressed his arm. "You're all invited to the wedding, of course. I'd marry him tomorrow if I could."

"Why not?" Harry said. "I can marry you. I'm a qualified marriage commissioner, and Jace and Kat can be your two witnesses. Whaddya say?"

Kat kicked Harry under the table. Marrying people was one part-time job that she wished her uncle hadn't signed up for.

"What the hell—?" Harry frowned as he rubbed his knee. "That hurt."

Gia squealed. "Really? I had no idea you married people. That would be fabulous!"

Kat glanced at Raphael. For the first time she saw a hint of fear on his face. Would a real wedding make him run? He couldn't go far while aboard the ship. But that wouldn't last.

Kat frowned. "We're going to the cave tomorrow, remember?"

"We can cave in the morning and have the wedding in the afternoon." Harry turned to Gia. "As long as that works for you."

"Of course it does!" Gia clapped her hands together.

"But you don't have a dress or anything." Everyone ignored Kat as they focused on Uncle Harry who described the steps involved in a shipboard wedding.

They spent the next hour discussing wedding plans as they dined on a sumptuous feast of freshly caught salmon and salads and finished with dessert trays laden with tarts and cookies. The yacht was surprisingly well stocked for their impromptu trip.

Kat stood. "I really am tired. I'm sorry, but I'm headed downstairs to sleep."

Gia pouted. "Can't you stay for a little while?"

She smiled at Gia. "Not if I want to be rested for your wedding."

"I'll be down soon," Jace said.

"Take your time," Kat needed time alone to inspect the wallet's contents and learn more about the mysterious Anne Bukowski. She headed out on deck. It was dark now, the summer heat dissipated. A soft breeze fluttered her hair and reminded her how grateful she was to be freed from the cave.

If only she could free Gia from the clutches of Raphael.

Chapter 19

Kat had just powered up her laptop when the stateroom door handle jiggled. She had locked the door as a safeguard, not wanting any interruptions while she examined the wallet. She hadn't expected Jace back so soon. She gathered up the wallet contents and shoved them under her pillow and walked to the door.

She opened the door to find not Jace, but Gia.

Kat froze. While the wallet identification was hidden, the weathered wallet still lay in plain view on the bed. She hobbled to the bed and grabbed it.

"Sorry to make you get up. I just came to see how you're doing." Gia's gaze dropped to the wallet in Kat's hand. "Where'd you get that ratty old thing? Isn't your wallet red?"

She nodded. "This one isn't mine. I found it." Kat turned the wallet over in her hand.

"On De Courcy Island?" Gia plopped down on the bed beside Kat. "You're so lucky, Kat. You must have an eagle eye. I never find so much as a nickel."

Kat didn't bother to correct her. She couldn't exactly explain that she found the wallet in Gia's stateroom. At least not until she had more information. "I've got to locate the wallet's owner." She typed Anne Bukowski into the search box and pressed enter.

"I'm feeling a lot better now," she lied. She glanced at her laptop screen. She needed time alone to narrow down the dozens of pages of search results. "You really should go back upstairs with the others. I don't want to spoil your fun."

"You're not," Gia said. "I feel bad at how we left things. I know you don't think Raphael's right for me, and you're just being a good friend. But he's the real thing, and I've never felt this way about anyone. I love him and I'm marrying him no matter what you think. Can't you just let it go?"

"I'll try." Kat didn't even sound convincing to herself, but what else could she say? She glanced at the search results. She scanned the first page and saw nothing local, so she clicked through to the second page.

"I'm sure you're exhausted after what happened," Gia peered at Kat's laptop screen. "Maybe whoever lost it is still on the island. Raphael and I could locate the person tomorrow and return the wallet."

"Maybe. Let me see what I find first." No way in hell was Raphael getting his hands on the wallet. That only alerted her to another problem. "Do me a favor. Don't tell anyone I found the wallet, okay? Not until I find the wallet's owner."

"But why? What's the big deal?"

"I left out a part of my story," she lied. "The cave isn't the only place I got lost. I took another trail detour. Jace will kill me if he finds out. Promise you won't tell anyone, not even Raphael?"

"Sure, Kat. What else can I do?" Gia sat on the bed and sighed as she leaned against the headboard. She held up her hand and admired her ring once more.

Just dump your imposter boyfriend. "Nothing, I'm fine. I'll just rest a bit so I'm ready for your wedding tomorrow."

"I can't wait! It all feels like a dream to me. I have to keep pinching myself."

The only way to stop the wedding without hurting Gia was to convince Uncle Harry to delay it somehow. "Maybe I'll even be able to go to the island tomorrow. I'll show you the cave."

"Sounds like a plan!" Gia hugged her. "Just don't get us trapped, okay?"

Kat laughed. "Don't worry, I won't. I'm just relieved to be back."

Gia rose. "I'm glad you're feeling better. And thanks for trying to make things work with Raphael. I know you two haven't exactly hit it off. But you will. You two are so much alike."

"We're nothing alike."

"Yes, you are. You just don't see it yet. You're both in finance. You're an accountant and Raphael's a business expert. He's made so much money he has a hard time keeping track of it all."

Kat doubted Raphael did anything but track money, and his expertise lay more in exploiting people rather than business opportunities. "I just think you're moving too fast, Gia. You just met him. It's too soon to get married."

"I am getting married, Kat. Just because you're marriage-phobic is no reason for me not to follow my heart."

"I am not marriage-phobic. We're just not in any hurry."

"You and Jace have been together a long time. Make it official already." Gia clasped her hands together. "Why not tomorrow? We'll have a double wedding!"

"No, Gia." She and Jace would get married, but on their own time. She certainly didn't want her own wedding memories to be tinged with regret for Gia. "Following your heart doesn't mean ignoring everything else."

Gia frowned as she stood. "Are you saying that Raphael can't be trusted? Just because you don't like him doesn't mean that I can't."

"Whether I like him or not is not the point." Kat winced in pain as she followed Gia to the door. Her knee wasn't getting much better. "If he loves you, he'll still be here next week, next month, or next year. All I'm saying is that you should slow down and think this through."

Gia's spontaneity was one of her most endearing traits but also one of the most dangerous ones.

"He's the one for me. I've never been surer of anything in my entire life."

"That's good. Did he make you sign a pre-nup?" Gia hadn't mentioned one, but any billionaire's lawyer would insist upon it. The flip side was that Gia wasn't exactly penniless herself. With her salon and savings, she was doing well. Raphael could lay claim to half of Gia's assets. Gia probably hadn't thought of that.

Gia burst out laughing. "Of course not! Raphael would never ask me to do that. He knows I'm not after his money. What's mine is his and vice-versa."

"If that's the case, why does he even need your investment in the first place? I mean, being a billionaire and all."

Gia rolled her eyes. "He doesn't need it at all. He's doing me a favor by letting me in on it. Just like he is Jace and Harry."

Kat froze in her tracks. "Jace and Harry haven't invested anything."

"They have now," Gia said. "They just signed the papers."

"Jace wouldn't invest without discussing with me first." Gia was mistaken. She and Jace discussed everything as a couple.

"Well, he did, and so did Harry. Why is that such a big deal? They can think for themselves."

Kat bit her lip. She regretted leaving the dinner table. While the money was a big deal, the bigger deal was that Jace knew how she felt about Raphael, yet he invested anyway without telling her. "How much did they give him?"

Gia waved her hand. "Just the minimum, a hundred grand."

A small fortune, an amount that neither of them could afford to lose. Not that anyone could. Kat's heart pounded. Had Jace and Harry each invested a hundred thousand? Or maybe they had gone in together with fifty thousand each. Either way made her sick to her stomach.

"I told them to invest more, but they didn't. Jace probably didn't tell you because he knew how you'd react."

Kat's face flushed. She didn't want to have this discussion with Gia. "He might have mentioned something." Jace hid it from her because he knew she disapproved.

The only saving grace was that there were no banks nearby. Uncle Harry was old school and did his banking in person, not online. Jace was more tech savvy. Had he managed to get an Internet connection long enough to transfer his money?

"You'll see, Kat," Gia said. "Bellissima is going to pay off big time. But in the meantime, I need your help. Will you help me get ready tomorrow?"

"Huh?"

"You can help me with my hair and makeup. I don't even know what I'll wear yet. Will you help me?"

"Of course I'll help." It was the last thing she wanted to do. She had to delay the wedding somehow. "But why not wait and have the wedding when we're back in Vancouver?"

"What's to wait for? We just want a small wedding, no fuss. Onboard is absolutely perfect."

It wasn't what she expected from Gia, who loved splashy celebrations. "If you're sure that's what you want." Gia hadn't recognized the wallet, but somehow the mysterious Anne Bukowski figured in Raphael's plans. If she discovered how, it might be enough to stop Gia from a terrible mistake.

"What time is the ceremony tomorrow?" Could she expose Raphael in time?

"Four o'clock. We'll explore the cave in the morning, return to the ship for lunch, and have the afternoon to get ready. I can't wait!" Gia stood. "I'd better get back upstairs before Raphael comes looking for me."

Kat waited until Gia left. As soon as the door closed she clicked on the first entry and couldn't believe what she saw.

The local news headline read Bukowksi Family Vanishes into Thin Air. She clicked on the entry only to find that she had lost her Internet connection. She refreshed her computer connection to no avail.

Without the full article it was impossible to glean further details on the location, date, or even how or where the family disappeared. Bukowski was a fairly common surname, but without the story details she couldn't verify the family's first names. Was Anne Bukowski and her wallet somehow part of the story?

She retrieved her phone but the screen was dark. The battery was still dead from the cave and she had forgotten to plug in her charger. She sighed and plugged it in. Whatever secrets the story held would have to wait.

Chapter 20

Kat stood on the aft deck and shone her flashlight off *The Financier's* stern. It was highly unlikely that *The Financier* and Catalyst were identical twins. More likely than not, Raphael's yacht was stolen, and she intended to prove it.

The flashlight cast an uneven light in the dark. She craned her neck to get a closer look at the yacht's lettering under the dim flashlight beam. The Catalyst images on the Majestic Yachts website haunted her. The ship appeared identical to Raphael's, yet the shipbuilder's website described it as "one of a kind". Either there were two identical yachts, or *The Financier* had been renamed. Her hunch was that Majestic Yachts had built only one yacht, Catalyst, and that she was onboard it this very moment.

She refocused on *The Financier's* lettering. It appeared fine from a distance. But close up, even in the dim evening light, the white paint that surrounded the letters was a slightly lighter shade than the rest of the ship's stern. Had it been recently repainted? She leaned over the railing to get a closer look.

There was no trace of ghost lettering underneath, but one thing gave her pause. She hadn't noticed it until now, but the second to last letter, the e, was slightly crooked. She seriously doubted that a custom-built, multi-million-dollar yacht would have crooked lettering.

She bent over the railing and reached down towards the letters. She could barely reach the F. She scratched the lettering with her fingernail to see if there was anything underneath. But the enamel was thick and rubbery, not brittle enough to scratch under her nail. The paint's freshness was suspicious, and it was far too fresh for a six-year-old ship. Of course it could have been repainted recently, so the paint's condition didn't necessarily mean anything in itself.

But the uneven shading of the white paint and the crooked letter e almost certainly meant something.

Next, she studied *The Financier's* registration numbers and scribbled them on a pad of paper. She shoved the notepad in her pocket just as a deep voice boomed behind her.

"What are you doing?" Raphael stood just a few feet away. His arms were crossed and he looked angry.

Kat was so startled that she almost fell overboard. She managed to grab the railing and right herself. As she turned to face him, she noticed he was alone. "Nothing. Just checking out the aft deck." The notebook was now safely tucked away but she couldn't hide the flashlight.

"With a flashlight? Your curiosity knows no bounds, does it?" All pretense of politeness was gone.

She was at a loss for words. "I guess not." Raphael was so close she smelled the alcohol on his breath.

"Gia and I don't appreciate your negativity. If you know what's good for you, you'll stop poking around in our business."

"Gia's her own person. She's also my friend, and that makes her my business too. I look out for my friends." Since when did Gia need someone else to speak for her? Raphael was tightening his control by the hour, and Kat didn't like it one bit.

"You'd better watch yourself, if you know what I mean."

Kat ignored the threat. "I protect my friends, no matter what. If you know what I mean."

Raphael snorted. "The only person she needs protection from is you. Do I have to spell it out for you? Gia's mine, not yours. I can turn her against you with a couple of words."

"Don't threaten me." Kat straightened her posture. She was actually several inches taller than Raphael, the only advantage she had right now. "Gia can think for herself."

He chuckled. "Not anymore. She's happy with me making all the decisions now."

"That'll wear off soon enough, once she sees the real you. You don't fool me one bit, and Gia will see through you soon, too." He had trapped her in the cave intentionally. She wouldn't reveal what she knew, but she didn't have to be polite, either.

"Consider yourself warned. Back off." Raphael glared at her and blocked her exit, arms crossed. "Just watch yourself."

Kat brushed his shoulder and pushed past him. Raphael couldn't intimidate her, even if he had turned everyone on board against her. There wasn't anything she could do until they saw the truth themselves. She just hoped it wasn't too late.

Back in her stateroom ten minutes later, Kat's suspicions were confirmed. She typed in *The Financier's* call sign, or registration numbers, into the Canadian government's transport registration database. The database kept a legal record on all registered watercraft, including port of registry and legal owner.

Invalid result

That didn't prove or disprove Raphael's claim, since he would claim the yacht was Italian. But given what she saw on the Majestic Yachts website, the ship seemed to be North American.

Then she remembered Pete's comment. He had been hired on in Friday Harbor in Washington State, so the yacht was probably American. She navigated to the U.S. registration site and retyped the numbers. This time she got a match.

The result returned was not for *The Financier*, but for Catalyst instead. Finally, she had proof that the boat had been renamed. Since the ship's registration record was current under Catalyst, it appeared to be stolen and renamed. Raphael's story about sailing his live-aboard Italian yacht around the world was bogus. She could finally expose him in a lie.

She navigated to the Majestic Yachts website and checked that the Catalyst's registration number was still the same. It was. Since it was also listed for sale on the Majestic Yachts website, it was almost certainly stolen. That was easily proven with a phone call when the yacht company reopened tomorrow morning.

She rose and set her laptop on the desk just as Jace burst into the stateroom.

"What did you say to Raphael? I just ran into him and he's furious. He wants to go home immediately."

"Finally, some good news for a change." She placed her hands on her hips. "Gia told me you invested. How could you invest with that scammer and not even tell me?"

Jace avoided her gaze. "I was going to tell you."

"When exactly?"

"See, this is why I didn't say anything. He's not a scammer, Kat. He's the real deal. But I knew you'd give me the third degree."

"Of course I will. I'm the only thing standing between you and losing your money forever."

"I knew you were up to something."

"Jace, the only one up to something is Raphael. If you and everyone else weren't so blinded by the promise of riches, you would see through him in a second."

"I wasn't born yesterday. I know a good opportunity when I see it, and I'm not letting this one pass me by."

"Well, you just gave your money to a thief." She swiveled her laptop screen towards him. "Raphael's yacht is stolen, and here's proof. The registration number is for a yacht named Catalyst, not *The Financier.*"

Jace studied it for a moment. "There's got to be a logical explanation. Maybe he just bought it and the paperwork hasn't gone through yet."

"It's registered in Washington State, not Italy. How could he have just bought it when he claims to have sailed here from Italy?"

"Maybe he registers it in another country. Lots of ships are registered elsewhere, like cruise ships registered in Liberia and stuff."

Washington State wasn't exactly a tax or liability haven. "No one would do that."

"True." Jace scratched his chin. "But I'm sure he has a good reason. Let's ask him."

"No, Jace. You're completely missing the point. He lied about his so-called Italian ship and his trip halfway across the world. There's only one reason to change the yacht's name."

A flicker of doubt passed over Jace's face.

"It proves the yacht is stolen."

"That's crazy."

"No, giving him your money is what's crazy." Something was rotten aboard *The Financier*, and the sooner she exposed the truth the better. But it wasn't going to be pretty.

Chapter 21

Kat and Jace had finished breakfast by the time Uncle Harry appeared on deck. He emerged from the galley, his plate laden with scrambled eggs, toast, and sausage. A second plate was stacked with pancakes.

It had been a self-serve affair. Kat and Jace had cooked together, though they barely spoke. Kat was furious about Jace's secret investment, while Jace accused Kat of being on a witch-hunt.

"You're eating all that?" Jace stood and pushed back his chair. "So much for your fitness regime."

"I need my energy. Big day today." Uncle Harry sat opposite them and tucked a napkin into his shirt. His plate was heaped with food, a heart attack waiting to happen.

Kat raised her brows. "You mean the cave exploration?" Despite her previous experience and her still-sore knee, she actually looked forward to returning.

"That too, but I was talking about Gia's wedding. I've never married a billionaire before."

Kat frowned. "You can't marry them, Uncle Harry."

"Of course I can. I'm a licensed marriage commissioner." Harry paused with a forkful of eggs midair. "This will be my first wedding at sea! Or should I say, my first nautical nuptials?"

He swallowed his eggs and buttered his toast.

"That's not what I meant. I'm sure you'll do a bang-up job, Uncle Harry. It's Gia I'm worried about."

"Gia's fine. Been around long enough to spot people in love, and those two sure are. You're overreacting, Kat. If I didn't know you better, I'd even say you're a little bit jealous." Harry speared a piece of sausage with his fork.

Kat stole a glance at Jace, who raised his brows at her.

"That's ridiculous. I am not jealous." Just the only one who sees the truth. "I want Gia to be happy, but with the right man." Raphael didn't fit the bill. Her instincts told her he was far more than just the wrong romantic partner—he was a downright dangerous man.

"He's the perfect match. He's rich, and he loves her as much as she loves him." Uncle Harry grabbed the syrup carafe and smothered his pancakes.

"You sure about that, Uncle Harry?"

"Of course. Any fool can see they're in love. I've never seen her happier."

Jace cleared his throat. "Harry's right. Let Gia make her own mistakes. If that's what this turns out to be."

She glared at him. "Gia might be in love, but I'm not convinced Raphael is."

"She'll never do better than him. He's young, rich, and successful. A real catch for Gia." Uncle Harry's generation still held traditional views, and she had to bite her tongue not to respond. Gia didn't need to catch anyone.

"Did you ever consider that Gia might be a catch for Raphael?" Kat swallowed a mouthful of coffee. "She's self-made. She has her own business and is very successful."

"She's done very well for herself." Harry set his fork down and leaned back in his chair. "But he's ten thousand times richer than she is. Where's she gonna find another billionaire?"

"You never know." Everyone considered Raphael's yacht, designer clothes, and possessions as proof of his wealth, but it was so obvious the way he flaunted it that it was fake. "Besides, if they're so great together, why rush into anything? They have all the time in the world."

"Because I want to be the one that marries them, Kat. If they get married somewhere else, I won't be able to perform the ceremony. They're ready, I'm ready. What's the big deal?" Harry shook his head. "Marrying people is what I do for a living."

"You've only done one other marriage ceremony. Remember, this isn't about you, Uncle Harry." Now she understood: Harry saw this as his only chance to perform the wedding ceremony.

"Okay, so maybe it's a part-time job." He bit into his toast. "But it's the best job I've ever had. Watching a couple's expression when they tie the knot, and knowing I made it happen…it's priceless."

"Your job is very important, but there's a right time for everything. With Gia so caught up in her whirlwind romance, she might not be thinking clearly."

"I guess that's possible." He toyed with his food, dejected.

She needed further proof to convince both Jace and Harry. Without that, all she could do for the moment was delay the wedding. "What do we actually know about Raphael? We've known him for a day, he came out of nowhere, and he convinced Gia to invest money with him."

"When you put it that way it sounds bad. But look at all this." Harry waved his arm at the boat. "Proof he's successful."

"Maybe. But success doesn't make a happy marriage. Gia only met him a couple of weeks ago. Is that enough time to get to know someone?"

Harry looked crestfallen. "I guess not."

"You can still marry them later, Uncle Harry. I know Gia wants you to officiate, but let's convince them to hold off a bit. If they're meant for each other, it can't hurt."

"But what if they're traveling or something? This could be my only chance."

"I'm sure Gia will want you to perform the ceremony no matter what. She'd fly you in if necessary. Can you find some excuse to hold off for a day or two?"

Harry paused mid-chew. "All right. I suppose I can have a chat with her."

"No—don't do that." Kat's thoughts drifted back to the wallet in her pocket. It was somehow tied to Raphael since she had found it in his stateroom. Whatever the connection, her gut told her that it wasn't good.

"I just don't think Raphael is who he appears to be."

"Geez, Kat. You really got it in for this guy." Jace raised his hands in protest. He was still mad that she had questioned his investment decision. "What's wrong with Raphael? He's a great guy for letting me in on the business."

Kat's heart thumped in her chest. Jace still refused to disclose how much he had invested. That scared her. "I think you're making a big mistake."

Harry picked up his empty plate as he rose from the table. "Nah. The Bellissima hair straightener business is gonna make us all rich."

Kat grabbed his arm. "Remember your last big investment? You almost lost everything you owned." Uncle Harry had bought stock in a diamond mining company while Kat investigated the very same company. It had turned out to be a massive fraud, and he had been extremely lucky to get his money back.

"Go find Raphael right now and tell him to undo whatever you've done. You'll never see your money again unless you get it back now." Raphael had managed to bilk three of his four guests. They'd never see that money again unless she stopped him.

"Not a chance. I'm not missing the boat on this one."

"You'll be missing more than the boat, Uncle Harry. Where's the investment information? I want to see it."

Jace glared at her but remained silent.

Kat was dying to ask Jace the exact same questions, but it would almost certainly provoke an argument. She would wait until later when they were alone.

Harry shifted his gaze. "It's back in Vancouver. He'll mail it to me once we're back in town."

"You invested without reading the fine print?" Raphael had no intention of sending Uncle Harry anything.

Uncle Harry held his hands up in mock surrender. "I knew you'd say that."

"I thought this yacht was his office," Kat said. "Why isn't his paperwork on board the ship?"

"Dunno. He probably meant his lawyer's office."

"Did you sign anything?" Kat frowned.

"Nope."

"You didn't hand over any money?"

"Not yet. I can't get to the bank till Monday."

Kat sighed in relief. Thank goodness Harry was old school and didn't bank online. "Don't commit to anything else. Not until I check a few things out."

"Make it quick. I'm not missing my chance to hit the jackpot." Uncle Harry waved his arm at the boat. "Maybe I'll get a yacht too."

"You've already hit the jackpot. You've got a good pension and money in the bank. You always say you have everything you need. Why risk that?"

"Just once I want to get in on the action. Don't ruin my chance, Kat."

The odds of a missed opportunity were slim, but financial ruin was almost a certainty. The odds were stacked against everyone but Raphael, but she intended to change that.

Chapter 22

Kat was already on her third coffee by the time Gia and Raphael emerged on deck. Raphael grunted good morning at Jace and Harry, but simply glared at Kat. Gia glanced at Kat, then averted her gaze. Gia's eyes were bloodshot and swollen. She had obviously been crying and appeared again on the verge of tears.

Harry sprung from his chair and headed to the coffee machine at the bar. He poured two cups of steaming black coffee and handed one to each of them. "Good morning. Sleep well?"

Raphael muttered something under his breath and set his coffee cup on the table.

"Hmmph." Harry turned and disappeared into the galley. He returned seconds later with a couple of chocolate croissants. He offered one to Gia, who shook her head.

Jace's late night admission worried Kat. Not only had Jace invested all his savings, he had also added money from a line of credit. He now owed money on an investment that never existed in the first place. While it was his money, she felt betrayed by his actions. They significantly impacted them both, yet he hadn't even consulted her.

Kat shifted her gaze to Gia. Her disheveled appearance was uncharacteristic. She appeared tired and instead of her usual fawning over Raphael, she sat slightly apart. Something was amiss, since Gia barely looked at Raphael. Had she finally realized that Raphael was taking advantage of her?

"Eat up. I can't wait to go ashore and find the cave." Harry munched on the second croissant, oblivious to the tension around him.

"Change of plans, Harry," Raphael said. "We'll hold the wedding first and go to the island this afternoon instead."

Gia remained silent, though her lower lip trembled slightly.

Bad news, Kat thought. She had even less time to stop the wedding.

"Even better," Harry said. "I'll get changed. I wish I brought my suit."

"Hold on," Jace turned to Gia. "We've got lots of time for the ceremony. Wouldn't it be better in the afternoon?"

Gia shrugged. "Whatever Raphael wants is fine with me."

If Gia wouldn't change her mind about the wedding, Kat had to at least convince her to delay it. She'd think of some excuse once she talked to Gia privately. "If that's the case, let's go to your stateroom and get ready."

Ten minutes later, Kat sat on the bed in Gia's stateroom, no closer to convincing her to change her mind. Her gregarious, self-assured friend had morphed into a meek, insecure shadow of herself. She simply did whatever Raphael instructed. "What's a few more hours? The afternoon is much better for a wedding."

"It's not ideal, but Raphael wants to marry me as soon as he can." Gia pulled her hair back as she studied herself in the mirror.

Kat scanned the stateroom floor, hoping to find additional evidence tied to the wallet. She saw nothing other than shoes Gia had pulled out of the closet for consideration. She rose from the bed and walked around it as she pretended to stretch. Nothing visible on either nightstand either.

Gia pulled a half-dozen dresses from the closet and laid them on the bed. Most were brightly colored sleeveless dresses similar to the one she wore. "This is all I've got to wear. I always dreamt of a big wedding and imagined myself in a vintage wedding dress. These ones just aren't special enough. The whole thing just seems so rushed."

Kat nodded but didn't add anything.

Gia held a black sequined sheath against her body. "How about this one?"

"Don't wear black for your wedding." Kat shook her head. Though marrying Raphael did call for mourning. "Why can't you wait till we're back in Vancouver? I'll help you shop for a dress."

"We can't wait that long." Gia sighed. "We're leaving for Costa Rica tomorrow."

Pete had mentioned Costa Rica too.

"Costa Rica? Why? For how long?" If Raphael left the country he'd never come back. She seriously doubted he'd take Gia with him, though, no matter what he said. Gia probably didn't even have her passport with her.

"I don't know. It just depends on Raphael's business meetings. I wish I had time to plan a bit better. It's all kind of last minute."

"You can say no, Gia. You don't have to go."

Gia wavered momentarily, then shook her head. "Of course I'm going. I can't lose him. I'll never find a guy like him again."

Kat could hardly wait for Raphael to get lost, but she had to get everyone's money back first. "Just don't rush the wedding. You can fly into San Jose and visit him anytime. Or he can come here."

"He's not staying in San Jose. He's staying someplace remote on the west coast. It's only accessible by boat."

A strange place to conduct business, Kat thought. "If he can get there, so can you. It's not a big deal." She had visited Costa Rica several times. While the roads weren't great, you could still travel pretty much anywhere. It just took a long time.

"No, it is a big deal. If I want to help Raphael, I have to support him." Gia wiped a tear-stained cheek. "I know he earns more than I do, but why is it all or nothing? I have to leave my salon, my home and my friends, just like that." She snapped her fingers. "It's not fair."

"You're absolutely right. You shouldn't have to." It was totally out of character for Gia to abandon her livelihood and her clients at a moment's notice. "Why Costa Rica? It's such an unlikely place to launch a product."

"It makes no sense to me, either." Gia let out a sigh. "But he always knows what he's doing. I just wish I could get a straight answer out of him."

Kat put an arm around her friend's shoulder. "At least give yourself enough time to get your affairs in order. You've got to close your shop and make arrangements for your absence. There's no reason to rush into things."

"I don't want to say anything in case he changes his mind about me. He's the best thing that's ever happened to me."

More like the worst thing that had ever happened to her. "If Raphael won't consider your wishes, maybe he's not the right guy for you."

For once Gia didn't protest. "I wish we'd do what I want at least some of the time."

"Tell him. Starting with the wedding. We'll explore Valdes Island for a few hours first. Then we'll all be ready to celebrate."

"You're right." Gia drew in a deep breath. "It's time I put my foot down. We'll keep the wedding this afternoon as planned."

While Gia was still determined to marry Raphael, it at least bought Kat a little time. She headed to her stateroom, anxious to continue her research on the Catalyst and determine how exactly it came to be called *The Financier*.

Chapter 23

Kat had just a few minutes before they disembarked on Valdes Island, but it was long enough to power up her laptop and hope for a restored Internet connection. She typed Anne Bukowski's name into her browser's search field and clicked on the top result.

This time her connection was good and she was able to search several entries. There was nothing on Anne Bukowski, but there was a tragic story about a family named Bukowski several months ago. Their fatal boating accident had been front-page news, and she vaguely remembered hearing about it. She scanned the article to refresh her memory.

The story was dated July 1st, almost two months ago. The Bukowski family's partially burnt boat was discovered by a fishing trawler, abandoned and adrift in the Georgia Strait, halfway between Vancouver and Victoria. There was no sign of the family of three aboard the partially burnt boat, and they were presumed lost at sea. Frank, Melinda, and four-year-old daughter Emily had been en route to a new home in Victoria. A sad story, but one unrelated to Anne Bukowski. The family tragedy got her no closer to the wallet's owner.

The Bukowski name was nothing more than a coincidence.

Or was it? What were the odds of a missing family and a missing wallet with the same surname? That wallet belonged to someone, and Anne and Melinda could possibly be related. She clicked through the remaining articles on the marine accident and froze when she read the third article.

Anne Bukowski's full legal name was Anne Melinda Bukowski, though she preferred her middle name, Melinda. How had the missing woman's wallet ended up on board Raphael's yacht? Whatever the reason, it couldn't be good. At the very least, the wallet was an important piece of evidence. Raphael should have turned it over to the authorities. It could pinpoint the location of the missing family.

Anne Melinda's wallet had resurfaced, yet she and her family had vanished without a trace. What were the odds of her being without her wallet when she disappeared? Less than zero, since they were in the midst of moving from Vancouver to their new home in Victoria. A shiver ran down Kat's spine.

She pulled the worn leather wallet from her nightstand and studied it. The wallet was old, but both the wallet exterior and contents appeared undamaged by water or fire. How had it come to be on Raphael's yacht?

She opened the next article and was rewarded with a picture. The photograph showed an attractive thirty-something brunette with shoulder-length hair and brown eyes. She held a baby girl in her arms, probably Emily from a few years earlier. The woman smiled into the camera, but her resigned eyes betrayed her. Clearly she was trying to be happy but wasn't.

She had to do something about the wallet. She couldn't return it to Gia and Raphael's stateroom even if she wanted to. Gia had already seen her with the wallet in her stateroom, and she had lied about where she had found it. Gia would be furious if she admitted to snooping in her stateroom. Kat had accused Raphael of thievery; now she appeared dishonest herself.

She had to keep her discovery from Gia for the moment, since her confession would likely be shared with Raphael. There was no good reason for the wallet to be in Raphael's possession but plenty of sinister ones. She would turn the wallet over to the police when they returned to Vancouver tomorrow.

She shifted gears and looked for more information on the yacht. She checked her watch and realized that she should have used the time to call Majestic Yachts. She made a note to call once they returned from the island, once she could be sure of a few moments alone. Jace could walk in at any moment, and he would be angry about her fact-checking. In the meantime she would glean as much information as she could. She clicked on the first search result and found that her suspicions were correct.

The Catalyst had been stolen two months earlier from the Friday Harbor marina in the San Juan Islands, Washington State. The San Juan Islands were less than an hour away by sea. All she had to do was prove that Catalyst was really *The Financier*. She could finally expose Raphael in a lie.

Her pulse quickened as she reread the article on the Catalyst. The yacht had been moored in Friday Harbor by a wealthy family who hadn't used it since relocating to the east coast several months earlier. Since Catalyst was listed for sale, there was no crew onboard. Anyone spending a few days in the Friday

Harbor marina would have quickly noticed it was unoccupied. That made it easy to steal without attracting too much attention.

With the information from Pete and her search results, it was safe to assume the Catalyst and *The Financier* were one and the same. It also explained the yacht's motley and sparse crew and Pete's reluctance to answer personal questions.

Raphael wouldn't have risked hiring professional sailors. They would be difficult to find on short notice, and they would likely report the stolen yacht. They would almost certainly refuse to work onboard.

The stateroom door opened and Jace stepped in.

"Let's go," he said. "They're waiting for us on deck." Jace's dark mood from earlier had passed. He walked over and kissed her.

Gia had stood her ground and stuck to the afternoon wedding. Finally some good news.

"Come see this first." She handed her laptop to Jace so he could see the screen. She had the yacht manufacturer's website open. On it were two dozen pictures of the yacht, showing all angles of the yacht's exterior and most of the interior rooms.

"That's nice." He glanced at the screen and placed her laptop on the bureau. "Grab your stuff or we'll be late."

"No, Jace. Look more closely." She clicked on their stateroom. "Recognize this room? It's got the same furniture and bedspread as our stateroom."

"There's bound to be identical ships around."

"No, there isn't. This yacht was custom-made." She tapped on the description. "Everything from the wood used to the configuration of each stateroom was made to order."

"So what?"

"This yacht is stolen, and I think I can prove it." She navigated to the Canadian government registry site. "See those call numbers? When I enter the registration number on the site, nothing comes up. That's because this yacht isn't Canadian."

He looked at her blankly.

"I know what you're thinking, but this yacht isn't Italian either. Neither is Raphael. I can't prove he's lying about his identity yet, but there is one thing I can prove." She punched the registration numbers into the Washington State website and showed them to Jace. "This yacht is American. *The Financier's* call numbers belong to another yacht, the Catalyst."

Jace frowned as he studied the screen. "You sure you entered the numbers right?"

She nodded. "I've double and triple-checked." She described the ghost shadows under the yacht's name and the crooked e. "If, I'm right, then this yacht is stolen."

"And Raphael isn't the billionaire tycoon he claims to be." Jace was skeptical. "There's got to be a logical explanation. You're reading too much into things."

"About a stolen yacht? I don't think so."

A flicker of doubt passed over Jace's face as he peered at the screen. "You sure they don't build any two ships the same?"

Kat nodded. "Even if they did, the interior design would be different, since that's chosen to suit the owner. Look at the artwork on the walls." She pulled up the dining room picture and zoomed in on the artwork above the sideboard. "That's identical to the print onboard this ship. The paintings in our stateroom are exactly the same, too."

Jace walked over to the painting above the bed and traced his finger over the brushstrokes. "This is an original oil painting. One-of-a-kind. There's got to be a logical explanation."

"The logic says that it's stolen. Look." She enlarged the photograph of their suite and focused on the limited edition Salvador Dali print that hung above the bureau. "The Dali print is number three of 120. What does ours say?"

"Three of 120. Maybe it's a fake. Who would steal a yacht? Isn't that kind of obvious?"

"Not really. As long as he stays away from where the ship was stolen, who's going to recognize it? No one's going to check the vessel registration. There's more." She told him about the wallet and the Bukowski family disappearance. "We've got to stop him, Jace. Before it's too late."

Chapter 24

Raphael entered his stateroom and stopped cold at Gia's expression. One look and he knew he was in trouble.

Gia's eyes narrowed as she waved an envelope. "Tell me why you have plane tickets to Costa Rica. They're dated tomorrow, and one is in another woman's name."

Raphael waved her away. "Relax, bellissima. It's not what you think."

"Don't give me that crap. Who the hell is Maria, and why are you two flying first-class to Costa Rica?" Gia crossed her arms and glared at him. "I thought we were sailing there."

Raphael just shrugged and smiled. "My assistant got your name wrong. I'll get her to fix it."

"Nice try. How the hell do you get Maria out of Gia?"

"Static on the phone, I guess. We had a bad connection." Raphael fidgeted with his fingernails and avoided her gaze. Something or someone had triggered Gia's response, he was sure of it. For the first time there was doubt in her voice. He had to speed up his plans.

"How could you not notice? Those tickets are for a flight tomorrow, yet you said we're sailing there. Something doesn't add up."

"Plans change, bellissima. My business contacts postponed a few meetings, so I've got more time. Now we can sail on the yacht instead of flying." He stroked her hair.

She pushed him away. "You adapt to their plans, but not mine. Why should I close down my business and leave my whole life behind with a couple days' notice?"

Raphael shrugged. "It happened quickly. We can't ignore business opportunities."

"We seem to be ignoring mine." Gia frowned as she studied the ticket. "This ticket was booked a month ago. That's before we even met. Don't lie to me, Raphael. You planned to take someone else, didn't you?"

"Of course not."

"Then tell me why you're flying first class with a woman named Maria." Gia's eyes narrowed. "You keep changing your story. I don't like being lied to, so don't hold me responsible for what happens next if I find out you're lying to me."

Brother XII had it right, Raphael thought as he faced an irate Gia. The man had convinced thousands of followers to move to his stupid little island and hand over all their worldly possessions, and still he escaped scot-free. The Brother could probably give him a lesson or two on how to pull off a scam.

Unfortunately it was too late for that.

Brother XII had cut his losses and run when people asked too many questions. But unlike Brother XII, Raphael couldn't just burn down buildings and escape without a trace. The very people he was running from were aboard his ship.

Gia's sudden distrust stemmed from something or someone.

Kat.

He had invited Gia's friends aboard as potential investors, but that backfired when Kat started asking too many questions. If Gia was suspicious, no doubt they all were. He had to get rid of them, and soon. Things were spiraling out of control. If he didn't act soon he might lose everything.

His pulse raced. Was his passport in the envelope with the tickets? A simple mistake that could cost him everything. He couldn't remember.

"Bellissima, I—" His voice caught in his throat.

"Don't play games with me, Raphael." Gia tapped the envelope. "Who is she?"

"Maria is a former employee, the sales manager for Latin America. She quit a week ago. That's another reason I decided to sail instead of fly. I just forgot to cancel the tickets." He held out his hand for the envelope. "Give that to me. I'll get everything straightened out."

Gia hesitated before handing it over. "You better not be lying to me."

"Of course not, bellissima." He wrapped his arms around her and kissed her. "Now get your stuff together for our hike."

Gia broke from his embrace and obediently stuffed her pack.

If only Gia hadn't found the tickets. He hated messy endings.

Chapter 25

Kat sat on deck at the outside bar with Jace and Uncle Harry. Gia and Raphael were late again. Uncle Harry was antsy, anxious to go ashore. He fiddled with the remote and scrolled through the channels until the television above the bar displayed the all-news channel.

They waited for the couple and hoped their plans hadn't changed yet again. The Valdes Island tunnel trek was all Kat had left to look forward to. For a few hours at least, she could keep Raphael in her sights and prevent him from stealing any more from her shipmates. And delay the wedding that was certain to ruin Gia's life.

She half-listened to the news anchor as she rearranged the contents of her pack. This time she had packed all the essentials, including a flashlight and first aid kit. Her knee and ankle felt much better after a good night's rest. Some of the swelling had even gone down.

She tightened her shoelaces as the newscast cycled through the morning's top stories. Her ears perked up as the anchor mentioned new developments in the Bukowski disappearance. The name caught her by surprise, as she figured the family's accident was old news.

She jerked her head up to the TV screen. The camera panned across the water to a marina, where the remains of a burnt out boat was being towed.

The screen flashed to a news anchor who commented on the old news footage before he introduced the latest development. The screen flashed to a reporter on scene. He stood on the same dock as the earlier footage. This time there was no boat wreckage behind him. He pointed to the waters behind him as he described breaking news in the Bukowski disappearance.

Emily Bukowski's partially decomposed body was found today off the coast of Vancouver Island. The 4-year-old girl's body was discovered by a commercial fishing boat. The little girl had been missing for almost two months, along with her parents, Melinda and Frank Bukowski. No trace of her parents has been found to date. The Coast Guard continues to search in the area where the burnt out wreckage of their boat was discovered.

The RCMP consider the deaths suspicious. According to Melinda Bukowski's coworkers, she had recently quit her job after her husband, Frank Bukowski, accepted a teaching position in Victoria. Police checked all Victoria schools but were unable to locate the school that had hired Mr. Bukowski.

Kat shuddered at the thought of the little girl's body turning up in a fishing net. The television screen cycled through photographs of the Bukowski family. Her mouth dropped open in shock. "Jace, come here!"

Jace was busy loading his gear into the dinghy. "In a sec, I'm busy right now."

"But that's him! He's on TV." Kat jumped up from her seat.

"Who's on TV?" Jace's irritated expression changed to recognition. "What the hell is—"Uncle Harry noticed too. "Wow, the guy's a dead ringer for Raphael."

"No, Uncle Harry. That is him. Frank Bukowski and Raphael are one and the same."

Uncle Harry shook his head. "Nah, that's just not possible."

"I wish it wasn't." She had been certain Raphael was a thief, but the realization that he might also be a murderer made her blood run cold. "Whatever happens, don't let on that you know, okay?"

Uncle Harry nodded, though he remained unconvinced. "It's gotta be a mistake. The guy on TV is his twin brother or something. What's that called again?" He answered his own question. "A doppelganger."

"I doubt it, Uncle Harry." Her uncle didn't know about the wallet, but this wasn't the time or place to tell him. Melinda Anne's wallet had even greater significance now. Whatever had happened to little Emily appeared all the more sinister with the missing woman's wallet onboard.

Kat's handling of the wallet might have destroyed fingerprints and other critical evidence. She'd first move it to somewhere more secure than her nightstand drawer and then contact the police.

"I wonder what it's like to run into someone that looks exactly like you. It's like having an identical twin or something."

"I doubt that's the case, Uncle Harry."

"There's got to be an explanation." Uncle Harry scratched his bald head. "Can't we just ask Raphael?"

Jace stood transfixed at the TV screen as realization dawned on him, too. He started to speak just as Raphael suddenly appeared behind him.

"Ask me what?" Raphael was alone. His mouth opened into a smile but his eyes were cold.

Kat's heart thumped in her chest.

"Uh...you sure you're ready to get married?" Uncle Harry smiled. "Think before you leap."

Raphael laughed. "Of course I'm ready. I'm counting the hours. In fact, we've changed our minds again. We want the ceremony this morning. Can you do that, Harry?"

"I-I don't know." A sheen of sweat broke out on Uncle Harry's forehead as he stole a glance at Kat.

"Of course he can." Kat kept her tone casual, not wanting to raise alarm. They couldn't delay the wedding anymore without arousing suspicion.

"Good. You can marry us just as soon as Gia gets here. We'll go to Valdes right after the ceremony. We'll celebrate later when we return."

"I'll go help Gia," Kat said.

"No need. She'll be here in a couple of minutes." Raphael's eyes narrowed as he focused on the television. "Turn that thing off."

Kat broke into a sweat. Raphael had overheard at least part of their conversation. Had he seen the news story? If he suspected anything, they were in grave danger.

But Raphael's expression remained blank.

Harry switched off the TV and they spent the next few moments in awkward silence. Gia emerged on deck moments later in shorts and an oversized men's t-shirt. "Let's go."

Either Gia was starting a grunge wedding trend or Raphael hadn't informed Gia of the change in plans. She bet it was the latter.

Jace picked up on it too. "You're getting married in that?"

Gia shrugged. "No time to waste. Harry, you ready?"

"Wait—I forgot something downstairs." Kat motioned to Uncle Harry. "Can you help me with something?"

"I guess." He shrugged and followed her to the mid-ship staircase. "We'll never get anywhere at this rate."

"Relax, Uncle Harry. We need to talk." She glanced up at the surveillance camera above the staircase. She had to be careful until they were safely inside the stateroom.

Five minutes later she had briefed her uncle on everything she knew to date including the stolen yacht and Anne Melinda's wallet. Enough proof of Raphael's deception to convince anyone. And enough to make her very worried for Gia. She couldn't risk telling her friend yet, since any slip to Raphael could be dangerous for all of them.

"You think he killed his wife and daughter?"

"I don't know what to think, Uncle Harry. But consider the facts. He's claiming this stolen yacht is his, and says he's a billionaire. He's either a dead ringer for Frank Bukowski, or he is Frank. Since he has Melinda Bukowski's wallet, I'd say he's the real deal. With his daughter dead…" The gravity of their situation hit home. Money didn't mean a thing if their lives were in danger. "We're in big trouble. We're on a boat with a murderer."

Uncle Harry voiced the words she couldn't. "You really think he's a killer, Kat? That poor little girl. How could anyone do that?"

"I don't know what to think, other than we're in a lot of danger. We can assume the worst but hope for the best." She couldn't count on the latter, though.

Uncle Harry wiped sweat from his brow. "Did I just invest with a criminal?"

Kat nodded. "I'm afraid so."

"The odds of getting my money back are what?"

"Not great, but it's not over yet. We've got a bigger problem on our hands now. We can't let on about our suspicions, even with proof. We can't arouse Raphael's suspicions until we're safely off this boat. If he gets wind of what we know, he might do something desperate." Or deadly. Her mind raced. Was Pete merely an innocent bystander, or was he Raphael's accomplice? What about the rest of the crew? It was too risky to trust any of them.

Uncle Harry scratched his bald head. "We still need to prove he's the same guy, though. How do we do that?"

"You need identification to marry them, right? Ask him for it." He might not have any, or whatever he had might be an obvious forgery. It was all she could think of.

Gia was about to marry a cold-blooded killer, and Kat was powerless to stop it.

Chapter 26

The wedding ceremony was a somber affair, at least for Kat. If the situation wasn't so grave, the ceremony would have been comical. Gia looked like a vagrant in her baggy t-shirt and shorts. Raphael's Gap shorts and tank top weren't even close to Italian designer wear. "Fran—I mean—Raphael…" Uncle Harry's cheeks reddened as he tripped on his words.

Raphael's mouth dropped open but he quickly recovered.

Kat had confided in Uncle Harry as a last resort, in the faint hope that he wouldn't go through with the wedding. Her uncle wasn't much of a bluffer, and he was obviously conflicted. No wonder, as he was about to marry Gia to the very man who had robbed him blind.

"Raphael and Gia, we are gathered here—" The words caught as Uncle Harry cleared his throat. "Sorry."

He had to perform the ceremony or arouse suspicion. Kat and Jace also had to sign as witnesses. They had no choice in the matter. They were all essentially captive on the yacht now.

While they could physically leave, Kat couldn't lose sight of the man that had stolen their money.

Or killed two innocent people.

Raphael glared at him. "I thought you did this for a living?"

"I do. It's just that—I've been doing so many ceremonies lately that I got you mixed up with another couple." His face reddened. "Let's start again."

"Just get it over with." Raphael was the most irritable groom Kat had ever seen. And the worst dressed.

Gia looked at Uncle Harry oddly. "What about the paperwork? You didn't mix up any names there, right?"

Uncle Harry waved her away. "Of course not. Raphael showed me the marriage license. Both your names are printed on it. Which reminds me. I need to see some identification."

"But you've known me since I was eight years old," Gia protested.

"Procedure," Uncle Harry said. "I've got to follow the rules. Identification please. Both yours and Raphael's."

"This is the most bungled ceremony I've ever seen," Raphael said. "Why didn't you ask for our ID before?"

Harry didn't answer.

Gia rummaged through her purse and tossed her driver's license on the table.

Raphael handed an Italian passport and driver's license to Uncle Harry. "Why do you need my identification? I already provided it when I got the marriage license."

"Just crossing my t's and dotting my i's. Can I see that marriage license again?" Harry licked his finger and tabbed through his Marriage Commissioner handbook.

"You brought that with you?" Kat was surprised that her uncle had packed his handbook. Or anything at all, since he hadn't planned on a trip in the first place.

"Gotta do my job right."

Raphael sighed and pulled an envelope from the back pocket of his cargo shorts and extracted the marriage license. He handed it to Uncle Harry. "Can we start now?"

It was a brilliant stroke of luck. Uncle Harry wasn't exactly meticulous, but he took his Marriage Commissioner duties very seriously. Each minute he delayed bought them time to stall.

Uncle Harry studied Raphael's passport and recorded information from it in a small blue notebook. After an eternity he returned the document to Raphael and repeated the process with his Italian driver's license.

Raphael sighed. "We haven't got all day."

"What does it matter, Raphael?" Gia stroked his arm. "It isn't even ten o'clock yet. We've got all the time in the world."

Since Raphael and Gia already had a marriage license, they had obviously planned the wedding prior to the trip. The license was good for three months. Of course, a marriage license alone didn't mean that the couple had planned to have the ceremony on this trip.

Kat was disappointed that Gia, who told everyone everything, had omitted to mention their intended marriage plans until now. She had never known Gia to keep a secret from her before, let alone something this big. On the other hand, she'd barely had any time alone with her friend since boarding the yacht. Raphael had made sure of that.

Gia replaced her driver's license in her wallet. "Ready, Harry?"

Harry cast a nervous glance at Kat.

Kat shrugged. Raphael already had the marriage license, so no one except Gia could stop the wedding. Like that was going to happen.

"Okay, take your places." Harry motioned for Gia and Raphael to face him in front of the bar. Kat and Jace sat on barstools and watched while Raphael took Gia's hand.

"Let's do it." Raphael pulled Gia close and the couple faced Harry.

The ceremony passed in a blur for Kat. Why did Raphael need to marry Gia if he already had her money? As a fraud investigator, she regularly encountered scammers. They didn't stick around once they had the money, and within a very short time they disappeared forever. Clearly he had targeted Gia, but he also got Uncle Harry and Jace's money as a bonus.

Raphael was, at the very least, a yacht thief who had defrauded Gia, Jace, and Harry. At worst, a murderer. The wallet didn't prove that, but it was damn incriminating. The television news story left no doubt in her mind that Raphael was really Frank Bukowski. She had to contact the police without arousing Raphael's suspicions.

"Kat?"

"Huh?" Uncle Harry beckoned her to the bar where a file folder sat.

"Sign here—right on the witness line there." Uncle Harry tapped a forefinger on the paper. "Now it's all official."

She searched his eyes to see if there was anything she could do. There wasn't, so she scribbled her signature alongside Jace's. "Done."

"We're all legal then?" Raphael lightly punched Harry's shoulder.

"Yup. I'll file all the paperwork once we're back in town. You two just tied the knot. Congratulations!"

Jace pulled two bottles of champagne from behind the bar. "Let's celebrate." He filled their glasses.

"A toast to the happy couple." Harry's voice was uncharacteristically flat. "Here's to happily ever after."

More like happily never after. The couple were now married, and without a pre-nup, everything was community property. Gia's property was also Raphael's. Whatever he hadn't already gotten from her was half his now.

"Bellissima, my wife." Raphael lifted a lock of Gia's hair and whispered in her ear.

Gia sealed her own fate with a kiss on Raphael's cheek. She turned to face them. "I can't wait for Costa Rica and the next chapter of my life!"

Kat just hoped it wasn't the last chapter. She had no doubt that Monday morning was zero hour. Raphael would extricate himself from Gia and disappear, taking her money.

Kat had less than twenty-four hours to build a case against Raphael and get the money back.

And break her friend's heart in the process.

Chapter 27

The best-laid plans often go awry, and the De Courcy Island hike was no different. Immediately after the wedding ceremony, Raphael announced that they wouldn't be going ashore after all. Instead, they set sail for Valdes Island, where they would search for the cave and connecting tunnel there instead.

The Valdes Island cave wasn't exactly a well-kept secret. The cave's mouth was right on the beach, visible to anyone in the harbor. The entrance was at least ten feet wide, and even from thirty feet away Kat saw that it was tagged with graffiti. Judging by the empty bottles and garbage strewn around the entrance, it was popular with local partygoers too.

They cut across the rocky beach to the entrance. Pete and Jace were in front with Uncle Harry and Gia close behind. Kat trailed behind everyone and kept a close watch on Raphael. She was both surprised and nervous that he had invited Pete along. Pete claimed to be a casual worker, but maybe that was part of Raphael's bigger plan. She simply didn't trust anyone right now.

She couldn't afford to, especially since Raphael was almost certainly a murderer.

"Are you sure this is the place?" Jace walked slowly around the entrance. "It hardly looks like a secret." Logs surrounded the blackened remains of a bonfire that scarred the sand a few feet away.

"The entrance is well known to everyone," said Pete. "Locals party here, but they don't venture much further than the first cave chamber. The deeper chambers are blocked, but there is a secret passage."

Kat didn't think she could handle another secret passage, especially with Raphael lurking nearby. She motioned to Pete and Raphael. "You two go ahead. We'll follow."

Jace nodded while Uncle Harry bent down to tie his shoe.

"Suit yourself." Pete turned away and headed for the cave entrance. "We'll wait for you outside the second chamber."

"What are we waiting for?" Gia placed her hands on her hips. "Why can't we all go together?"

Kat didn't have an answer.

"We shouldn't all go together for safety reasons," Jace motioned them over to the circle of logs. "Two groups are better than one."

Kat brushed dried kelp off one end of a log and sat down. Harry, Gia, and Jace followed suit.

"What's the big deal? I thought the cave was safe," Gia turned to Jace. "Why is Raphael going first instead of you? Since you're the search and rescue expert and all."

Jace frowned. "This isn't a search and rescue; it's just common sense. No one even knows we're here exploring the cave. All the crew knows is that we're exploring the island. If we get lost and no one knows about the hidden chamber, then we're all in trouble."

"We'll let them go ahead," Kat added. "No point in a bunch of us charging inside and getting into trouble." Jace was a genius to think of the accident angle. Raphael's eagerness to explore the cave gave her the creeps, especially after her earlier close encounter. She wasn't going near the cave with him around.

"Okay." Gia sighed as she sat down on a large boulder. "I never wanted to explore the stupid cave in the first place. It's the last thing I expected to do on my wedding day."

"At least you've got a nice honeymoon to look forward to," Harry said.

"Lucky me." Gia sighed and stared off in the distance.

"Cruising down the west coast to Costa Rica is a lot better than what those Brother XII women experienced," Harry said. "That guy destroyed a lot of lives. Fooled more than one woman, too."

"You got that right," Jace said. "He used Mary Connally's money to buy 400 acres right here on Valdes Island. He also bought three islands in the De Courcy group. To add insult to injury, he used her money to buy an engine for the tugboat he ultimately escaped on. Even though he left her and everyone else stranded, she said she'd finance him all over again.

"Then there was Myrtle. She failed to do what a so-called goddess of fertility should do; produce offspring. It turned out that Myrtle wasn't fertile after all."

If Jace realized the irony of his story, it wasn't apparent by his expression. Two women had been duped by a man. A century later, the same story played out with Gia and Raphael. Love is so blind.

They sat silent for a few minutes. Though no one said so, Brother XII's story had lost its cachet now that they had their own mess to deal with.

Pete and Raphael hadn't returned, and even Jace and Uncle Harry were reluctant to follow in their footsteps. Raphael had sensed a change in the air, and his reaction to Uncle Harry's slip-up during the wedding ceremony worried Kat.

"Brother XII sure destroyed a lot of lives," Uncle Harry said. "Sounds like he pretty much ruined everybody he came in contact with."

"He wasn't the only one," Jace said. "His third mistress wasn't a victim like the other ones were. Mabel Scottowe was also known as Madame Zee. She was more like a sadist, and Brother XII was happy to let her run the show. She was a cruel overseer and struck people with her bullwhip at the slightest provocation. The followers weren't much more than slaves at that point. They were hardly fed, and the women were forced to haul 100-pound sacks of potatoes. They worked from 2 a.m. to 10 p.m. every day."

"They should have just refused," Harry said.

"Impossible," Jace said. "He threatened to send the husbands and wives to separate islands. What would you do?"

"I wouldn't fall for any of that," Gia said. "I hate to say it, but it just serves them right for being so gullible. Who would let themselves get duped like that?" She shook her head.

"You'd be surprised. The smartest people were fooled. Apparently Brother XII was very charismatic. Somehow he still found new followers and the money kept flowing in, even after he was exposed as a criminal."

"Not very smart," Gia said.

"No, but some crooks are very convincing," Kat said. "I can't imagine letting someone treat me that way."

Jace shot her a warning look as Raphael and Pete emerged from the cave. Neither looked happy.

"Why didn't they all just gang up on him and escape?" Gia shook her head. "I can't believe they would spend years slaving away like that."

"Don't forget the whole mysticism angle. Aside from having no way of getting off the island, they truly believed their souls would be destroyed. Besides, where would they go? They had nothing but the clothes on their backs." Kat glanced at the two men, who had stopped just outside the cave. Raphael gestured angrily to Pete, who just shook his head. They were still out of earshot.

"It's astonishing how so many people can be controlled by one man. They were totally brainwashed. Someone figured things out eventually, right?" Harry poked at the charred firewood with a stick.

"Not until it was too late." Jace shifted his position on the log. "They didn't want to believe they were tricked. They were all smart successful business people, so even admitting to themselves that they had been taken in a scam was difficult. They were ashamed.

"They didn't realize the extent of his deceit even after he took everything of value from them. It wasn't until he had set fire to all the buildings and disappeared on the tugboat that they came to terms with what had happened."

"Couldn't they catch him and bring him to justice?" Gia asked.

Jace shook his head. "He transacted everything in cash, remember? No paper trail. And there were no photographs of him, either. Cameras weren't exactly common in those days, but he was a well-known person. Yet he flew into a rage if anyone tried to take his picture. Too bad. I would have liked a photo for my story.

"There are some drawings of him, though. He had a satanic-looking goatee, not exactly a fashion trend at the time. He looks a bit ridiculous, like a devilish magician. Probably trying to look like a mystic or something."

"Those poor people," Gia said. "If only they had a crystal ball to see into the future. They never would have gotten messed up with that guy."

"What are you guys doing here?" Raphael's face was flushed. "We've been waiting inside for you."

"I'm not going in some dark cave, Raphael." Gia's lower lip trembled like she was on the verge of tears. "This isn't my idea of a wedding celebration."

"We'll celebrate later." His voice had a hard edge to it. It sounded more like a command.

Uncle Harry stood. "I want to go back to the boat. I'm tired."

Raphael looked behind him, but Pete averted his gaze.

Whatever had transpired between the two men wasn't light conversation. Judging from Pete's body language, he wasn't entirely in sync with Raphael. He appeared angry that they hadn't entered the cave. Regardless of whose side Pete was on, at least they weren't outnumbered.

Kat's gut did a somersault as Raphael sat down on Gia's right. Pete rested on a log a few feet away.

"Brother XII got away with all that gold." Uncle Harry tried to lighten the mood. "That crook won in the end."

"Smart guy," Raphael kissed the top of Gia's head.

"I don't know," said Jace. "A smart man wouldn't have angered so many people. He had a good thing going until greed got the better of him. Some say he actually left the gold behind."

"I guess people have searched for it?" Uncle Harry asked.

"Yes, all over the island, including the site where his house was. No one's found it, although they did find a note hidden under some floorboards."

"What did it say?" Gia asked.

"For fools and traitors, nothing."

Raphael wasn't the only one with a gift for manipulation.

Chapter 28

They walked back towards the dinghy. Kat was anxious to return to the ship. Raphael's yacht was the only place she felt safe, and the irony of it didn't escape her. Somehow the CCTV cameras onboard comforted her, but that was ridiculous. If the cameras were actually monitored, the stolen boat would have probably been recovered by now.

"You guys are really missing out," Pete said. "You come ashore but don't even bother to check out the hidden passage. Hardly anyone has ever been inside. Who knows, maybe the treasure is hidden there."

Jace stopped mid-step. "I thought you said the passage was blocked."

"It is, but I know how to get in. There's enough of us to move the boulder out of the way. We'll need everybody to help, though."

Jace shrugged. "Sure, count me in."

"Me too," Uncle Harry said.

"I'll pass." Gia glanced at Kat for agreement.

Kat nodded. She didn't blame Gia one bit. It was already late afternoon, and caving didn't exactly make the activity list for most new brides on their wedding day. Had Gia finally recognized Raphael's self-serving nature?

Gia tapped her watch. "We'll wait an hour, no more. After that, we're returning to the ship."

Kat felt a surge of hope as the old Gia replaced the meek diluted version. The time alone gave her a chance to reason with Gia, though she hesitated to reveal much of her findings. Gia's loyalties hadn't been tested yet and you never could tell when love was involved. "We'll wait on the beach."

The men turned and headed towards the cave single-file. Pete and Jace were closely matched in height and size, though Pete was probably twenty pounds lighter and on the skinny side. Raphael was at least six inches shorter, but easily outmatched Uncle Harry in size, strength and youth.

Gia kicked at the sand. "How can he expect me to leave everything behind?"

A loaded question Kat had no intention of answering.

"I love Raphael, but I find some things about him really annoying. Like how he makes all the decisions for both of us. At first I liked the idea of someone taking charge and taking care of me, but he doesn't even consider what I want half the time."

"Maybe you should object more often."

"I'm afraid to. Married or not, he might get tired of me. He could replace me just like that." She snapped her fingers. "He's got the world at his fingertips. He can have anyone he wants."

"You're not exactly helpless, Gia. You're also not doing yourself any favors with those comments. Do you really think he would replace you?"

"I kind of do. At first his whole world revolved around me, but now I just feel like an afterthought." Her lower lip trembled. "We've only been married a couple of hours. What will it be like in a few years?"

Raphael would never stick around that long. That was Gia's saving grace, though she didn't know it yet. "You didn't think of that before you married him?"

"It all happened so fast. It's like a fairytale or dream that I didn't want to wake up from. And he said we'd turn my salon into a franchise, yet now I'm shutting down my salon. Our plans change by the minute. What would you do if you were in my shoes?"

"I wouldn't go. I would never give up my dreams that easily. The right person wouldn't expect you to, either." Kat drew in a deep breath. "There's something I need to tell you, Gia. There are some strange things going on aboard the ship."

"I know you don't like him, Kat. Let's leave it at that."

"This is different. I can't tell you unless you promise not to discuss it with Raphael. You could put all our lives in danger."

Gia chuckled. "Don't be so dramatic. We're all perfectly safe."

"I'm serious. Do I have your word?"

"Sure."

"Raphael's yacht isn't really called *The Financier*. The real name is Catalyst. It was stolen from a marina recently. It's an American boat, not Italian, and I can prove it." She described the painted over name and the registration records. "I can show you the Catalyst write up when we're back on board. The yacht's exterior and interior are identical, right down to identical original oil paintings."

"There must be a mistake. Raphael sailed from Italy on *The Financier*."

"Raphael saying so doesn't make it true, Gia. My proof says otherwise." Gia would almost certainly confront Raphael about Melinda's wallet, so she refrained from mentioning it. The yacht was enough proof that Raphael was a liar.

Gia sighed. "Actual proof? Are you sure?"

Kat nodded. "He either stole it, or knows it's stolen. There's simply no other explanation."

"He lied to me." Gia jumped to her feet and made a beeline for the cave. "I'm gonna kill that bastard."

Kat chased after her and grabbed her arm. "Gia, wait. We need a plan. You can't do or say anything to let on that you know. Just act normal and we'll figure out what to do next."

"Do Jace and Harry know?"

"Yes, I just told them. I don't know what it all means. But we've got to be careful. He might be lying about other things. Let's go find the guys and get back to the ship."

They walked across the beach towards the cave. Gia's trust was key to their safe return. Amid the doom and gloom, Kat finally saw a glimmer of hope.

Chapter 29

Despite Kat's best intentions, she was once again inside a cave without a flashlight. She had forgotten amidst their on-again, off-again plans. "Jace?"

Her voice echoed through the cavern, but there was no reply.

"He's probably in too deep to hear you," Gia said.

Exactly as Kat had feared. Now that Raphael had locked up both Jace and Uncle Harry's funds, they were of little use to him. As potential victims, they were more like a liability. Accidents could happen inside the cave and without witnesses, no one was likely to find them in a little known chamber.

"Jace?" She shouted this time. If the cave exploration had been a ruse to separate Jace and Harry, they didn't have much time. She walked faster as her eyes adjusted to the darkness.

"Pretty cool in here," Gia switched on her phone's flashlight beam. The dim light was a vast improvement. "I think I hear Raphael's voice."

They inched along the corridor as a male voice grew louder. They followed the curved walls and about a minute later Raphael appeared. He clutched a rock tightly in his right hand.

Kat pretended not to notice, but her heart raced. There were two of them against Raphael. Or against Raphael and Pete, who had just emerged from the shadows. Was the rock in Raphael's hand a souvenir or a weapon? If it was the latter, he could seriously hurt them. Had he purposely separated them from Jace and Uncle Harry?

Gia faced Raphael. "Why didn't you answer Kat when she called?"

Raphael ignored her. He turned the rock around in his hand, deep in thought.

"Where are Jace and Harry?" Kat scanned the cavern but saw no trace of them. Raphael stood in the center of the passage and blocked the way forward.

"They went on ahead," Pete stepped in front of Raphael, just a few feet from Kat. "We haven't seen them for at least fifteen minutes."

Fifteen minutes was a long time. Despite the cool cave interior, a thin sheen of sweat broke out on her forehead. Neither Jace nor Uncle Harry would voluntarily separate themselves from Pete and Raphael. Jace would never go off on his own in an unfamiliar cave. He also would have returned within the promised hour. Something was amiss with Jace and Uncle Harry; she just knew it.

"What's that rock in your hand, Raphael?" Gia grabbed his arm and tried to pry the rock from his hand.

"Leave it." He tightened his grip and pulled his hand away. "I collect rocks."

"A rock hound," Gia said. "I didn't know that about you."

"There's a lot you don't know." Raphael turned back towards the entrance. "Let's get out of here."

Gia's eyes widened but she said nothing.

"Wait a sec. We can't just leave Jace and Uncle Harry." Kat recalled her earlier cave experience. The men could have made a wrong turn. Their absence meant they were lost, injured, or somehow unable to retrace their steps.

"There's only one way out. It's not that hard," Raphael said.

"But it's an undersea tunnel," Kat protested. "There are at least two different passages. What if there are more chambers? They could be anywhere."

"I'll go look for them." Pete shone his flashlight beam ahead as he retraced his steps in the opposite direction. "Wait here. I'll be back in a couple of minutes."

Kat breathed a sigh of relief. Pete seemed cooperative. Even if he had sided with Raphael, at least danger wasn't imminent. She leaned against the cool cave wall and tried to appear casual.

She studied Raphael. The veins on his arms bulged as he kept the rock in his grip. She inched a little closer and was alarmed to see a red discoloration on the rock. The red stain was not only on the rock, but on his palm. She caught Gia's gaze and nodded towards Raphael's hand.

Raphael was nonplussed by Pete's decision, but that didn't necessarily mean anything.

For the second time in twenty-four hours, she was in a cave with a murderer. One way or another, it would be the last time.

Chapter 30

The red-tinged rock turned out to be nothing more than a souvenir, an archeological artifact.

"You should put the rock back where you found it," Kat said. The rock's crimson markings appeared to have been made with the same primitive paint that she had seen on the stone altar on De Courcy Island. It was paint, not blood, and it was probably thousands of years old.

"What difference does it make? Nobody visits this stupid cave, so no one's going to miss it." Raphael's eyes narrowed. "Besides, I don't like people ordering me around. I'll do what I want."

"That's not the point. This is a historic archeological site. You can't just take stuff." The Coast Salish artwork on the cave walls and boulders had stood unmolested for thousands of years. Raphael probably wouldn't even the keep the rock, but he saw nothing wrong with disturbing the site.

"I can, and I will. Maybe I'll even get more." He pulled out his pocketknife and wedged it into a crevice in the cave wall. He scraped at the rock and fragments fell to the ground. He pried the rock away with his hands and extracted a second, smaller rock. Another cave painting ruined.

Kat remained silent, aware her comments only aggravated his actions. She felt some satisfaction that Raphael had lost his cool, though. Still, she was relieved when Pete emerged from the darkness, followed by Jace and Uncle Harry.

"How did you even know about this passageway to start with?" Jace asked. "You grow up around here?"

Pete nodded. "My grandfather was Edward Arthur Wilson, better known as Brother XII."

Pete was about fifty years old, so it was possible, Kat thought. It also explained his local knowledge.

Jace whistled. "I had no idea. Why didn't you mention anything earlier?"

Pete shrugged. "I didn't want a negative spin put on things."

Harry tapped Pete's shoulder. "He must've been some guy. I mean, to convince all those people to follow him and all. There's two sides to every story, right?"

"I wouldn't know, since I never met him. He left the colony when my mother was only five years old. She didn't know her father very well either. My grandmother told us lots of stories about life in the colony, though."

"Which one was your grandmother? Mabel Scottowe?"

Pete shook his head. "My grandmother's name was Sarah. She was just one of many women he took advantage of. He and my grandmother never married, which was pretty scandalous at the time. She was left penniless and destitute like the rest of his followers. Obviously he wasn't a great guy, but he was still my grandfather."

"Understood," Jace said. "My story isn't so focused on the personal side as it is on the Aquarian Foundation and the rumored buried treasure. People love reading about stuff like that. I'd love to hear whatever you know about him."

"There's not much to tell that isn't already known. My grandfather believed that he was the reincarnation of the Egyptian God, Osiris. Together with a reincarnated Isis, he would father the New World Teacher who would lead the Aquarian Foundation in the new age. My grandmother was just one of many women who fell for his ridiculous story."

"It's an incredible story," Jace said.

"Whether he really believed it or not, I don't know. But that's what he told everyone."

"Maybe we can talk some more back on the ship." Jace smiled. "He must have been quite a character."

Pete shrugged. "I only know what my mother told me. Probably not what you're looking for, since I never knew him personally."

"Still, I'll bet those are some stories," Harry said. "What I wouldn't give to have been there."

Kat raised her brows at Harry but remained silent.

"Probably better not to be there." Pete shook his head. "My mom was born on De Courcy and lived on the island till she was fifteen. She's gone now, but she always told me stories about growing up. She didn't remember much of the cult, but when you grow up in a cult, that's all you know. For her, it was normal. There was one thing she always talked about. My grandmother worked twelve hours a day, with no time for my mother. It was hard, back-breaking labor. My mom thought that was a normal life until she left. But even as a kid, she was horrified by Madame Zee."

"Wow," Kat said. "Why didn't you mention any of this before?" Raphael probably knew Pete's local connection since he had almost certainly shared the reason for the trip with Pete, his crew member. Despite its relevance, Pete hadn't mentioned it on the trail yesterday.

"I don't want my family history written up in a newspaper article. Brother XII wasn't exactly honest, but he was my grandfather. It happened a long time ago and there's no one left but me now. Still, I don't want my family name dragged through the mud."

"I wouldn't do that," Jace said. "I'd run it by you first. A lot of people would be fascinated with your family history. The locals must recognize your name."

"They don't. Brother XII changed his name a few times, but anyone that knew him under other names is long since gone. Since he never married my grandmother, she didn't take his name. Aside from that, the cult members weren't locals anyways. People came from all over the world, and when the cult dissolved, they all left. The lucky ones scrounged enough money to return to wherever they came from.

"Everyone except my mother, that is. She couldn't even scrape two pennies together, so she had no choice but to stay. She worked as a maid till the day she died at sixty from cancer. She never knew anyplace else."

"How tragic," Gia said. "How did he get away with taking everybody's money?"

"He didn't completely get away," Jace said. "Some of the Aquarian members took Brother XII to court. He had purchased all of the colony's property with members' money, yet all the property deeds were in his name only. They managed to get the property deeds transferred from Brother XII into their names, but it was too little, too late. He had long since vanished, probably with money he had hidden away. Mary Connally got the deed for Valdes Island, since it was purchased with her money. It's long since been subdivided and sold, of course."

"At least that's something," Gia said. "Though it doesn't make up for all the abuse they suffered."

"Nothing can make it right," Pete added. "Maybe someday I'll tell all I know. But that day hasn't come yet."

Kat felt a chill down her spine as she realized Raphael no longer stood at Gia's side. He must have turned back towards the cave entrance. "It's getting late. Let's get back to the ship and the wedding celebration." The wedding was the last thing in the world worth celebrating, but at least it allowed her to keep a close eye on Raphael. She couldn't let him out of her sight. Their future depended on it.

Chapter 31

It was late afternoon when they finally returned to *The Financier*. The dinghy cut through the glasslike water as shadows danced across the boat's wake. All was serene on the water's surface, but tension brewed on board.

The cove was starkly beautiful, the silence broken only by the cries of eagles circling overhead searching for a meal. Perhaps they mistook Raphael's yacht for a fishing vessel and were hanging around for some of the spoils. A fishing vessel of another kind, Kat thought. No net to snare its victims, just a smooth-talking con.

"Watch this." Raphael threw the painted rock into the ocean. It skipped once before it sank in dark waters. He laughed. "Should've got more."

The archeological treasure was lost to the ocean floor, where it would remain, undiscovered and unknown forever. No one would know of its existence. Another piece of history hidden and forgotten.

It was all Kat could do to remain silent. There were even higher stakes involved if she antagonized Raphael. She had to keep her silence and composure if she wanted to live to see Raphael brought to justice.

They neared the yacht. She nudged Jace and pointed to *The Financier's* lettering on the hull. In the bright sun it was impossible to see any letters underneath the white paint, but the telltale crooked e was clear as day.

Jace wore a blank expression as he studied the yacht's name. It contrasted sharply with the yacht's exterior finish and the painstakingly handcrafted interior. One crooked letter didn't make a con, but it waved a major red flag. It was always the smallest of details that ultimately exposed crime, and this one stared them right in the face.

Gia followed Jace's gaze and frowned. She pulled slightly away from Raphael, who didn't seem to notice.

Kat's eyes met Gia's. Her friend wore a panicked expression. It wouldn't be long before her emotions erupted. She had to get Gia alone before it was too late. "Let's get dressed up tonight. Your simple shipboard wedding doesn't mean we can't have an extravagant after-party." She stood and motioned for her friend to follow.

"That sounds like fun." Gia's voice was oddly flat as she boarded the yacht.

Even Raphael noticed. "We'll celebrate however you like, bellissima." His sinister stare from a half-hour ago had been replaced by laughter, but his cold eyes still focused laser-like on Kat. He didn't even try to hide his contempt.

Ten minutes later they sat at the outside bar with cold drinks and snacks as they waited for dinner. Kat and Gia planned the rest of the evening, but it was almost impossible to stay focused while she watched Raphael for any sign of action.

Raphael stood and headed inside without a word.

Kat watched him leave, wondering what he was up to. His abrupt mood change worried her. He no longer bragged about his business or showed any interest in the Brother XII mystery. He was a man preparing his exit. She glanced at Jace, who wore a worried expression.

Uncle Harry grabbed the TV remote and switched to the all-news channel. A camera panned across a familiar seascape. Kat recognized Active Pass from her many ferry trips from Vancouver to Victoria. The TV reporter stood on a rocky beach and pointed to the water behind him.

"Melinda Bukowski's body was discovered by beachcombers early this morning. Police aren't commenting other than to say that a full autopsy will be performed."

A shiver ran down Kat's spine. The autopsy results from the little girl hadn't been released yet either. She had no doubt that both autopsies would reach the same conclusion: homicide. Regardless of the results, Raphael had some explaining to do about the wallet and the boat. Had he just found the wallet and kept it, like the rock from the cave? Highly unlikely.

What were the odds he had the wallet in his possession, yet was uninvolved in Melinda and Emily's demise? The probability was exceedingly small. In fact, together with his uncanny resemblance to Frank Bukowski, the likelihood was almost nonexistent.

She caught movement out of the corner of her eye. As if he had heard her thoughts, Raphael had returned to the bar. He stood transfixed by the television.

She quickly averted her gaze, not wanting to arouse his suspicion. Her face flushed with the thought that she now held a dead woman's wallet. She wished she had left it where she found it. But if she had, she would have remained unaware of Raphael's dark secret.

Only Jace knew about the wallet, but Raphael had probably noticed it missing by now. If he had been careless about hiding it before, he almost certainly would be looking for it now. Still, it would be a stretch for him to assume she had found it. Then again, maybe not, if he had seen her in his stateroom. Whatever the case, a family had gone missing nearby under suspicious circumstances, and Raphael had a wallet belonging to one of them. A coincidence that defied explanation.

"Sad about the little girl," Jace said. "And now the mother too."

"Tragic." Raphael was expressionless. "Let's go inside. It's getting cool out here." Without waiting for a reply he switched off the TV and walked inside.

Kat glanced at Gia, willing her to stay.

A shiver ran down Kat's spine. Raphael couldn't do much as long as they all stuck together. He was outnumbered. But he was also desperate, and since they were aboard a stolen boat with a thief and a murderer, they had better take precautions. The worst-case scenario wouldn't apply as long as Raphael remained unaware that they knew his secret identity.

Best-case scenario was that Raphael would simply run away. He already had all their money. Depending on what the autopsy results were, he had every reason to run regardless of what she and the others knew. He already knew what the results would show.

He also had every reason to fight to the death.

No one followed Raphael inside.

Uncle Harry pressed the remote and switched the TV back on and turned up the volume.

Kat froze as she watched the screen. A TV reporter stood on the beach with the ocean behind him. The camera panned along the beach to show a dozen or more police, coast guard and other personnel who scurried back and forth across the sand between the seaside road and the dock where the Coast Guard boat was anchored. Two uniformed men emerged from the ship carrying a stretcher. The reporter's voice-over described how the body had washed ashore. The body was badly damaged by the sea, but given the location and state of decomposition, it was assumed to be Melinda Bukowski.

Raphael had to be brought to justice.

At any cost.

She turned to Jace. "We need a plan."

He nodded. "That guy's definitely a flight risk."

"What are you guys talking about?" Gia's brows knitted together as she glanced at the television. "Tell me what's going on."

Kat didn't want to tell her. Gia's reaction could give everything away, and then Raphael—and their money—would be gone forever. On the other hand, the idea of her friend sleeping with a murderer was unthinkable. Raphael had every reason to silence those who might expose him.

Gia's face reddened. "Either you tell me right now, or I go straight to Raphael. I have a right to know, Kat. Whatever it is."

Kat pulled her chair closer. Gia was right. Jace and Uncle Harry already knew, so it was unfair to leave Gia in the dark. It was a huge risk, but one Kat had to take. "Remember what I told you about the yacht being stolen? Well, there's more." She told Gia everything.

It was going to be a very long night.

Chapter 32

Gia stood and stamped her foot. "He lied to me! I'll kill him."

"No, wait." Kat grabbed her friend's arm. "You can't say anything, Gia. We're already in danger." She motioned to Gia to sit down.

"You can't be serious. That's not the Raphael I know."

"That's the point, Gia. The Raphael you're in love with doesn't exist. Everything about him is one big giant lie." She repeated the evidence against him, from the stolen yacht to the wallet. Her friend needed to hear it twice to absorb it. "We've got to do something. The wallet I found onboard belongs to the woman in the TV news story."

Gia shook her head. "There's got to be an explanation. Can't we ask Raphael directly? Even if he is a thief, he's not a murderer."

"No. We don't know the extent of his involvement and how that wallet came to be onboard. Anything we say will hurt us.

At the very least, you'll never see him or your money again. At worst, you won't see anything again. We'll all be dead."

Gia rocked back and forth in her chair, clearly traumatized. "You think my husband is a murderer?"

"We don't know that for sure, but he's somehow involved. Why else does he have the wallet?"

Gia shrugged. "He probably found it on a beach or something."

"Maybe, maybe not." Jace added. "The Bukowski's had a fire onboard their boat. Yet the wallet has neither fire nor water damage. How likely is that?"

"Let's assume the worst and hope for the best," Uncle Harry said. "At least about the wallet. As for the rest, we are on board a stolen yacht, so we better assume that Raphael knows something about it."

"You can't just assume—"

"Gia, his whole story of sailing over from Italy is a lie," Kat said. "The boat was stolen a month ago in Washington State. I've already proven Raphael lied about that. What else is he lying about?"

A tear trickled down Gia's cheek. "I can't believe I just married a liar and a thief. How could I be so stupid?" She buried her face in her hands and sobbed.

"I'm sorry." Maybe telling Gia had been a mistake. Raphael would take one look at her and know he had been exposed.

Gia lifted her head and glared at Kat. "More importantly, why the hell didn't you stop me?"

Kat couldn't have stopped her no matter what, but Gia couldn't see that so she just shrugged. "I'm really sorry, Gia. I should have done more."

"What do we do now, Kat?" Uncle Harry scratched his head. "We're in cahoots with a criminal. We're on a stolen boat. What if we get arrested too?"

"We won't," Kat said. "We're also Raphael's victims."

Uncle Harry looked crestfallen. "Oh, right. He's got my money. Maybe we should just jump ship."

"We can't let him get away," Kat said. "Not only does he have your money, but he's got a dead woman's wallet and no logical reason for having it."

"Can't argue with that," Jace said.

Kat leaned in and lowered her voice. "We've got to get the yacht out of here and notify the authorities. We need an excuse to return home early."

"Like a mechanical problem or something?" Uncle Harry asked.

"Something like that, although I don't see how we can fake that." She still couldn't figure out if Pete was part of Raphael's scheme or not. "Maybe one of us could pretend to be sick or something. It has to be bad enough for us to return to port early."

"I could do that," Gia said. "For real, since I'm just sick about my money. Will I ever see any of it again?"

"If we get back in time, maybe." Kat wasn't entirely confident. "Scammers usually move the money out of reach pretty quickly. But there's always hope."

"At least we've got hope," Uncle Harry echoed.

A slim hope, but slim was better than none. Kat feared it might already be too late. "Here's what we're going to do."

Chapter 33

"We're not going back early." Raphael had no intention of ever returning to Vancouver. It was too risky. His picture was plastered all over the local news and he was certain to be identified. He patted his jacket pocket. Everything he needed was inside. His passport, money, and banking passwords. Time for a fresh start.

Gia pulled her clothes from the closet and threw them into a duffel bag on the bed. "We have to go back. You sprung this Costa Rica trip on me way too suddenly I only brought enough meds for a weekend. I can't go without more medication."

"You can get everything there, bellissima." He hadn't seen her take any medication and had no idea what it was for. He didn't really care, either.

"No, Raphael. I've only got one more day's supply. I need enough to last the entire sailing, plus a few more days for insurance. We've got to go back." Gia wrapped her arms around him. "It won't take long."

Any delay was too long. "I'll get your meds couriered to our next port of call. Problem solved."

"No, Raphael. Besides, I need to wrap up some business with the salon. It'll just take a couple of days. We've got to sail back to drop off Kat, Jace, and Harry anyways." She pressed her cheek against his chest. "Hey, what's in your pocket?"

"Nothing. Leave it alone."

"What kind of talk is that?" Gia stepped back and looked up into his eyes. "You're hiding something."

"I'm not hiding anything."

But Gia's hand was already in his pocket. She extracted the envelope before he could stop her.

His heart raced as she opened the envelope. It contained three passports, plane tickets, and enough cash to keep him under the radar for a few months.

She pulled out the plane tickets and studied them. "What's all this? Hey, who's Frank Buk—"

"Give me that." He snatched the envelope from her grasp and stuffed it back in his pocket.

"Let me see it." Gia pulled the envelope from his pocket again. She ran over to the bed and dumped the contents on the damask bedspread.

His heart sank as she grabbed a passport off the bed and flipped it open.

"Why do you have these?"

"Hand it over, Gia." His fake passport was in the envelope along with his real one. He'd had no choice but to keep his real identity since the Costa Rican bank accounts were under his real name. He hadn't yet moved the money to the account under his new identity.

She ignored him.

He should have left the country sooner, but he hadn't expected to score so big with Gia and her friends. He now had enough money to live a comfortable life in Costa Rica. He never had to work another day in his life. Once safely there, he would be out of reach and untouchable.

"Who the hell is Frank Bukowski?"

If she didn't know already, she would soon His name was plastered all over the news, with the discovery of Melinda's body. He had to get out while he still could.

"Raphael? Answer me."

He had two other passports. One under Raphael and another under a Spanish name. He should have ditched his real passport, but worried he might need it, even though he planned to use the fake ones. He would enter Costa Rica through a small seaport. There his passport would be only visually inspected, not electronically scanned. His fake identification should easily pass scrutiny, unless someone recognized him. As long as he didn't act suspicious, he was home free.

"I'm keeping it." Gia held her arm up high. "At least until you tell me who Frank Bukowski is, and what you're doing with his plane ticket and passport."

Raphael exhaled. "Long story for another day." He scrambled to invent a story. At least Gia hadn't opened the passport to see his picture, so she hadn't made the connection. Apparently she hadn't seen the television coverage either. His one saving grace, but one that wouldn't last. As long as he stayed calm, no one would get suspicious.

"No, Raphael. We're business partners and now we're married too. You can't hide things from me."

"It's not what you think, bellissima." He outstretched his arm to hers but she swatted it away.

"Don't lie to me." Tears streamed down her cheeks as she studied the tickets. "Two plane tickets to Brazil? What's this all about?"

"I don't know what you're talking about. I haven't lied to you about anything. Why would I lie to my wife?"

"You didn't answer my question." Gia held up a ticket up and studied it. "Like Maria and who knows who else. You're cheating on me."

Raphael laughed, relieved that Gia hadn't guessed the truth. "You know I would never cheat or lie to you, bellissima."

"I don't know anything of the sort. You're lying to me right now." Gia pulled off her ring and threw it onto the bed. "You won't even tell me the truth."

"Only because that would ruin my surprise for you." His mind raced to invent an excuse. He had let greed get the better of him. Still, the trip had been much more profitable than he had anticipated, since he had investments from more than one person on board. His luck had almost run out, though. He'd better run while he still could.

Gia stopped whatever she was about to say and wiped a tear from her eye. "What surprise?"

"The tickets are for my cousin Frank and his wife. I bought them so they could fly to meet you. Now I've ruined your surprise."

"But I don't understand. They live in Italy, not Canada." Gia's forehead creased. "Why do you have their plane tickets?"

"The tickets are just copies because I paid for them. My cousin already has their tickets." It was a stretch but Gia believed pretty much anything he said.

"But these tickets say Vancouver to Rio de Janeiro. We're going to Costa Rica. How can I believe anything you say when you keep telling me different things?"

"I booked the tickets before the Costa Rica meeting came up." Gia must have rifled through his pockets, which meant she suspected something. He tapped his forehead. "I forgot all about them. I'll have to change them."

Gia stared blankly.

"I want you to meet them, but since we won't be in Italy for a few months I thought this was the answer." He flashed what he hoped was a meek smile. "They're just dying to meet you."

"They are?" Gia dabbed at her tear-stained cheeks.

"I can't stop talking about you, so naturally they're curious." Raphael held his arms open. "Now come here."

Gia rushed to his arms. "Oh, Raphael, I'm so sorry. How could I have not trusted you?" She buried her face in his chest. "I feel terrible."

"No, I'm the one who should be sorry. I realize now how it looked." He was so good at this improv bullshit that he even impressed himself. "I'll think things through more next time. But that's only part of the surprise."

"There's more?" The corners of Gia's mouth turned up into a smile. "I never really doubted you, but I couldn't figure out who those people were. I guess I jumped to conclusions."

Gia was so gullible and believed his lie. That bought him some time, but it was clear that he'd better make his exit sooner rather than later. That Brother XII guy had it right. He took what he could and knew when to quit. The easy money wasn't so easy anymore.

"Just one thing, bellissima. Our tight schedule means we can't return to Vancouver after all."

"But what about the others? We have to take them back."

"We'll drop them off in Friday Harbor tomorrow morning. I'll arrange for a charter flight back to Vancouver from there." He had no intention of returning to the port where he had stolen the yacht, but Gia didn't need to know that.

"But Raphael, my meds, remember? I need them. It only takes a few hours to get back to Vancouver. We could always leave earlier."

He shook his head. "My personal physician will arrange everything. Your meds will be delivered to the ship when we dock in Friday Harbor." He patted her plump bottom. Gia's extra fat probably made her more buoyant than Melinda had been. He'd have to weigh her down enough to sink. "Just write down what you need, and I'll send it to him."

"But Vancouver's just a short detour. I don't understand why we can't—"

"Relax, bellisima. Everything's taken care of." A few hours from now, his problems would be gone forever.

Chapter 34

Gia searched Raphael's closet while Kat stood guard at the door.

Kat studied her friend. "You really scored with those passports. You sure you didn't give anything away?"

"I really don't think he did it, Kat. Even if you're right and he is Frank Bukowski, he's not a murderer. He can't be." Gia paused, her hand in a pocket as she searched Raphael's clothing.

"The facts don't lie. Normal people don't have multiple identities. I always thought his name was made-up. Now we have proof." Raphael Amore sounded like the name of a bare-chested hero in a bodice-ripper romance novel.

"What's wrong with Raphael Amore? It sounds so romantic. Gia Amore sounds so much better than Camiletti. And I don't want to keep doing this." Gia protested. "Every new find just depresses me more."

"Better the devil you know than the one you don't." Kat didn't blame Gia one bit. A whirlwind romance, wedding, and betrayal all within a few weeks. It was the stuff bad movies were made of. "Once you're finished with the clothes, check his shoes, especially under the insoles."

"His insoles? What could he possibly hide there?"

Kat shooed Gia back in the direction of the closet. "I'll finish the rest of the drawers. Then we'll check under the carpet."

"You've done this before. Since when do fraud investigators rifle through peoples' closets?"

"All in a day's work." They had no time to waste. Raphael could walk in at any time and catch them in the act.

"I always pictured you punching calculator keys," Gia said. "If my life wasn't being ruined, I might even find this a little bit fun."

Kat would rather search everything herself and spare Gia the pain, but there wasn't enough time. Gia wasn't the most detailed person, but she was completely focused on the task at hand.

Kat's only worry was Gia's waffling over Raphael. He still held power over her and played on her emotions. She yearned for his version of the truth so badly that she had overlooked some pretty blatant lies and evidence right in front of her nose. However, she cooperated when Raphael was out of sight, albeit reluctantly.

The stateroom search wasn't just about incriminating Raphael. She had to ensure there were no hidden weapons in the stateroom. Kat also held out hope that she might find other damaging evidence against Raphael. If it materialized, Gia could be convinced once and for all that Raphael was a fraud. Kat also hoped to find bank records to recover the money, but that was a long shot. Worst case scenario was that if the money was already gone, the bank records at least proved the crime.

Their search had yet to reveal anything. "You're in denial, Gia. He's already got your money, what about your life? We're all in danger until we get off this ship."

"We'll just leave in the dinghy. Problem solved."

"It's not just about us. Running away doesn't bring him to justice."

"That's not up to us." Gia sniffed.

"If not us, then who? Think about that little girl. He killed his own daughter. Not to mention his wife. Why would you be any different?" As long as Gia was doubtful and stayed with Raphael, she faced almost certain death. "We can't let him get away."

"He won't. I still don't believe he's a killer though. There's got to be a logical explanation for everything. Maybe he's not really Raphael, but whoever he is, I still love him, Kat. I know it's stupid, but I can't help it." Gia's voice broke as she handed the passport over to Kat. "Even with this."

Kat's mouth dropped open. "You said he snatched them back from you."

"He did. But I fished it out again later while he was distracted. He was so focused on making things up to me that he didn't even notice my hand in his pocket."

"Gia, you're a genius. Where did you learn to pickpocket?"

"Let's just say I'm a woman of many talents." She sighed. "I sort of wish I didn't grab it, though. Deep in my heart I know you're right, but I don't want my dreams ruined more than they already are. There's probably more than one person with the name Frank Bukowski."

"Better to know about it than not. At least you can protect yourself." Kat flipped the passport open to the photograph page. Raphael's face stared back on Frank Bukowski's passport. "You can't still have doubts, Gia."

Gia shook her head. "I know he's a fake. But I hope even the fake Raphael still loves me. Maybe this is his twin or something. He did say Frank was his cousin…"

"Nothing about him is real, Gia. You've fallen in love with a person that doesn't exist." She pointed to Frank's passport photograph. "See that cowlick? In his hair it's exactly the same. What about the birthmark? It's identical to his."

"Probably not." Gia's shoulders sagged. "I guess I don't really know him at all. How could I be so stupid?"

"You're not stupid. You were smart enough to get his passport, and you also picked the right one. That was a stroke of genius. Now that we know he's a fake, we know what to do. He can't get away."

"He still can, since I only took one passport. If I took the others he would have noticed for sure."

"It might be a passport for Raphael Amore." Most fraudsters didn't go as far as to get a fake passport, though you could easily buy one if you knew the right people. But most con artists weren't cold-blooded killers.

Gia's lower lip trembled as she slowly sat down on the bed. "How did I fall for him? I feel like such a failure. I've mortgaged my salon and given that jerk all my savings. How will I ever recover?" She pounded the mattress with her fist.

"We'll find a way," Kat doubted her words with every new tidbit of information. Raphael—or Frank—appeared to be a cold-blooded killer with a carefully thought out plan. A plan they were all now a part of.

Gia stood and paced. "I'm not letting him get away with this."

Gia's thirst for revenge would have been helpful earlier. Now her vendetta could jeopardize their safety. In retrospect they were lucky to be unaware of Raphael's true identity until now. "If we confront him, he'll kill us too."

"I at least want my money back. Is there any hope of that?"

"Maybe." Kat seriously doubted it. "How much did you lose exactly?"

"Enough that I'll have to work till I'm eighty, just to pay it back."

"I'll figure something out." Kat sighed. They had already spent twenty minutes in the stateroom searching. Jace was keeping Raphael busy with questions, but that wouldn't last long. "We should go on deck. Raphael will be wondering what we're up to."

"He thinks we're looking at clothes."

"We are."

"My clothes, not his." Gia sighed. "Can't you just hack into his account or something?"

"We don't have enough time for that. Even if we did, I doubt the money's sitting in a bank account under his real name." Kat paused. "We'll let the police worry about that, but first we've got to remove any means of escape." Once they were sure he had no access to weapons, they would lock him up onboard.

Gia grimaced. "I can't believe I married that jerk. I'm such an idiot for believing everything."

"You're not alone, Gia. It could happen to anyone." Kat checked her watch. "Let's finish our search." She turned to the bureau drawers. She was on the third drawer when she felt something wedged into the drawer back. She tugged on it and was rewarded with a cardboard box the size of a cigarette package. She opened it and couldn't believe what she saw. "Gia, look at this."

Gia almost fell backwards. The box contained six diamond rings, all identical. She glanced at her hand and then back at the box. "They're just like my engagement ring. Why does he have all those rings?"

Kat raised her brows. "I'm sure you have some ideas." The diamond-and-platinum rings were breathtaking, each with a two-carat diamond solitaire. A folded paper was wedged in the bottom of the box. She pulled it out and unfolded it. The invoice was for seven cubic zirconia silver-tone rings from a company in Hong Kong. She replaced the paper in the box. Gia's heart was already broken, no need to make her feel even worse.

Gia's fake engagement ring was proof enough. Raphael was just like every other slime ball fraudster she saw in her fraud investigation business. She could spot them a mile away with their flashy cars, designer clothes, and extravagant gifts. Always bought with someone else's money.

"You mean he targeted me from the start?" Gia gasped. "My whole whirlwind courtship was premeditated?"

Kat nodded. "I don't know how he found you, but I know why. Your savings, your successful business."

"He stalked me? That bastard!" Gia's voice rose and she broke into sobs. "I guess I mean nothing to him."

"Gia, keep your voice down. We don't want him walking in here."

Gia was finally convinced. That was good, because a wronged Gia with a vendetta was a powerful secret weapon she wouldn't wish on her worst enemy.

Gia wiped her tears on her sleeve as her expression brightened. "At least we can recover some of the money with these rings." Gia looked hopefully at Kat.

Silence.

"Even the rings aren't real?"

Kat nodded.

"He doesn't love me, does he? He probably doesn't even like me." A single tear fell from Gia's eye. "I'm just one of many women, aren't I?"

"I'm afraid so. We've got to stop him." The stolen money was the least of her worries. Raphael—or Frank—had already committed the most heinous of all crimes by murdering his wife and daughter. His latest wife was undoubtedly his next victim.

"How can I keep this to myself?" Gia stomped her foot. "I want to kill him."

Kat finished with the drawers and turned her attention to a corner of the carpet that had been pulled away from the baseboard. She slowly pulled it back, wondering if Raphael had used it as a hiding place for documents or, possibly, money. "You have to hold yourself together, Gia. Even if you have to count the hours. Say something now and he will get away with his crimes, I assure you." He'd also commit more.

"Get away with what?" Raphael stood in the doorway, arms crossed. He glared at Kat.

Kat jumped to her feet and shuddered. She hadn't heard the door open.

"Y-you're back already?" Gia stuttered as she jerked around to face Raphael. "I thought you were upstairs." She let out a nervous laugh. "We're just talking about—"

"How some people are tidy, and some aren't." Kat finished the sentence. "For instance, me and Jace. He's neat as a pin, and I'm messy. He's always picking up after me."

Raphael interrupted. "Why were you lifting the carpet? Did you lose something?"

"Kat's just helping me look for my earring."

Kat's heart thumped so hard in her chest that her shirt moved with every heartbeat. She was grateful for Gia's quickly thought-up excuse. One hand still rested on the carpet she had pulled up. She froze, afraid any movement might reveal her actions.

Raphael walked over and studied Gia's earlobes. "I see both your earrings. You're wearing them."

Caught in the act. A thin sheen of sweat broke out on Kat's upper lip.

Gia poked a finger at his chest. "Not the ones I'm wearing, silly. Other ones."

"Which ones?"

"My emerald and diamond stud earrings. I was showing them to Kat when I dropped one. I have to find it." Gia pulled a box from her purse and surreptitiously flicked one earring with her fingernail. It fell to the bottom of her purse.

"I hate losing things." Raphael stroked Gia's chin. "I'll let you get back to it. Just don't take too long. I've got a surprise for you on deck."

Kat shivered involuntarily.

"We'll be up in a couple of minutes." Gia kissed him on the cheek. "Back to the search."

"Suit yourself." Raphael backed towards the door.

Kat waited until Raphael's footsteps receded down the passageway. "Very convincing."

"Thanks." Gia beamed as she held out her purse. "Seriously, though—I have to find that earring in the bottom of my purse. Before we do any more searching."

"Sure."

Gia dumped her purse contents on the bed and sifted through the items one by one.

"Found it." Gia fished out the stud earring and held it up for Kat. "Now what?"

Kat held her forefinger to her lip. "Go through his stuff in the bathroom. See what you find."

"Like what? Another passport?"

"You never know. Maybe you'll find some cash, or checks or something. Don't forget he's hiding things from you while you are in the same room. The bathroom is a perfect hiding place. Look where you would never think to look."

"Well if he's hiding it from me, why hide it anywhere in here?"

"Because he needs to retrieve it quickly if necessary. He can't leave things in common areas onboard like the kitchen—"

Gia corrected her. "Galley, not kitchen. I am so going to miss not having a yacht. Why can't things work out with him?"

"He's a thief, remember? Would you rather go to jail with him, Gia?"

Gia shook her head. "I just want my money back. I should have listened to you in the first place. Although it has been fun."

"It's all an illusion, Gia. I'll bet this yacht costs a fortune in fuel. Where does the money from gas come from?"

"You think he's spending my money?" Gia's mouth dropped open.

"I don't think, I know. The sooner we stop it, the greater chance we can recover whatever's left."

"Good point." Gia's shoulders sagged as she disappeared into the bathroom.

Men often hid things in a basement or garage, but neither existed on a ship. His hiding place aboard the yacht was probably somewhere he could control access and retrieve his items quickly. Common areas were accessible by the crew and guests, so his stateroom was the only logical choice.

Gia emerged from the bathroom. One look at her face told Kat she was upset again. "What's wrong?"

"I'm not touching it. Come see."

Kat followed Gia into the bathroom where the toilet tank lid stood propped against the wall. She peered into the tank and swore under her breath. A plastic bag was wedged inside. From what she could see, the contents included a rope and several pairs of latex gloves.

A murder kit.

Had he used them on his family, or were they intended for future use?

Gia cowered by the door. "What the hell is all that stuff?"

"I have some ideas, but none of them good. Did you touch it?"

Gia shook her head.

"Good. Just leave it there and put the cover back."

Gia did as she was told. "I can't stay in here with him, Kat. What if he tries to kill me?"

"We'll figure something out." One way or another, tonight would be the last night aboard for all of them.

Chapter 35

Kat stood at the bow and scanned the horizon. The forecast called for a thunder and lightning storm, highly unusual for the coast in late summer. The water was completely still, as if waiting for the storm to hit. The late afternoon sun hid behind the low cumulus clouds that had closed in an hour ago. They brought with them an oppressive gloom and silence. Even the seagulls had stopped flying.

She glanced behind her, where Gia and Uncle Harry huddled around the table. The mood wasn't exactly celebratory. In fact, it was downright tense. If Raphael hadn't already noticed, he soon would. A change was in the air in more ways than one.

Uncle Harry turned his head and glanced at Kat. "What are we gonna do, Kat?"

She glanced over at the bar, where Raphael mixed drinks. "Just play along for now. I'll go below deck in a few minutes. Wait ten minutes and tell everyone you're sick. Then meet me in my stateroom." Jace sat at the bar talking with Raphael. She couldn't debrief Jace in time, but he was certain to catch on once Harry left.

Raphael brought a martini for Gia and beers for everyone else. Kat thought it odd, since he hadn't asked them what they wanted. And he had taken a long time to mix just one martini.

Gia held up her drink unenthusiastically. "Cheers."

A murderer who had already staged his own death had no reason to stick around. He wasn't likely to leave them unharmed, either. While they hadn't witnessed his crime, they had seen evidence of it

Kat and Gia's stateroom search had yielded no further surprises. The murder kit alarmed Kat, but at least they hadn't found other weapons in the stateroom. Finding nothing provided comfort that at least some areas of the ship were safe, though there were plenty of other hiding places they hadn't searched. Things would escalate quickly once the truth was exposed, and Raphael's change in behavior indicated a confrontation was coming.

She just wished she knew more about Pete's relationship with Raphael. Was he a partner in crime, or just a hired hand?

As if on cue, Raphael rose. "I've got to go. The crew says there's a problem." He kissed Gia on the cheek and headed towards the bow of the ship.

Kat hadn't seen any of the crew lately, and Raphael hadn't answered his cell phone. Probably just a ruse. She shivered involuntarily. "Let's go inside."

"I'm going to my cabin," Gia said. "Suddenly I don't feel so well."

*****

An hour later Kat, Jace, and Uncle Harry sat inside in the living room, transfixed in front of the TV monitor. Thunder rumbled outside and lightning forked across the sky. The storm was in full swing.

The 6 o'clock news anchor sat in front of a backdrop of the charred Bukowski boat and gave a recap of the missing family.

Seconds later the screen flashed to a police press conference. A police spokeswoman stood behind a podium flanked by several male uniformed police officers. "The coroner has ruled Emily and Melinda's deaths as homicides. Frank Bukowski's whereabouts are still unknown. The police are anxious to speak with anyone who was in contact with the Bukowski's prior to their disappearance."

"Do you consider the husband a suspect in their murders?" asked a woman off-camera. "Eighty percent of the time, it's the spouse, isn't it?"

A loud male voice rose above the others. "Is the fire the official cause of death? How did they die?"

The spokeswoman dismissed them with a wave of her hand. "No more questions today. We will update you tomorrow afternoon with any new developments." She switched off her mic and exited from the podium as the reporters shouted questions.

The screen switched to a fiftyish balding male reporter who stood in a studio with a backdrop scene from two months ago with the Bukowski's burnt-out boat. The charred hull was the only part of the vessel still intact.

"The police won't comment on cause of death, other than to call it suspicious. Frank Bukowski is still missing, though the police have not yet named him as a suspect."

"Given the suspicious circumstances, though, it's important to note what the police did not say." He pointed towards the ship's burnt out skeleton. "The arson experts we consulted said the ship's burn pattern indicates that an accelerant, like gasoline, was used. Secondly, whoever started the fire was on the boat."

Jace and Uncle Harry exchanged nervous glances.

Kat pulled out her cell phone and was dismayed to see that she had no cell phone signal. They would have to deal with Raphael until service was restored long enough to call for help.

The camera panned back to the reporter for a close-up. "Police refuse to speculate whether any of that suspicion extends to Frank Bukowski, or whether he is also a victim of foul play. In situations like this, the spouse is always a suspect. With Bukowski still missing, it's unclear if he is still alive. However, it is telling what the police are not saying."

Kat grabbed the remote and switched off the television. "We can't let Raphael catch us watching this stuff. If he knows we've unmasked his identity, he'll be forced to act." She still thought of him as Raphael and not Frank, despite what she now knew. "I hope Gia's okay. Maybe I should check on her."

Jace shrugged. "She's probably just resting. Give her some time."

"We need a plan to get through the next few hours," Kat said. "And convince him to return to Vancouver."

Jace shook his head. "He'll never go back. He's a wanted man and sure to be recognized."

"Then our only choice is to disable him," she said. "But what about the crew? I don't think Pete and the others are in on Raphael's scheme. But what if they are?"

"Then we're badly outnumbered." Uncle Harry scratched his head. "There's five of them including Pete. Raphael makes six. Against the three of us, four including Gia."

The exterior door swung open and a gust of air blew into the room, followed by Raphael. He stood by the door. "Who can give me a hand? We've got a leak."

Kat frowned. The yacht hadn't moved from its anchor, and it was unlikely the late-model yacht was in any sort of disrepair.

"Doesn't the crew normally take care of things like that?" Harry asked.

"They already have their hands full trying to contain the leak." Raphael stepped back towards the door. "Hurry. The ship could sink."

Kat met Jace's gaze. If it was true, they couldn't just stand by. They had no choice but to follow Raphael. If it was a trick, they had to spring into action much sooner.

"Let's go," Jace motioned for Kat and Harry to follow.

Kat trailed behind the others as they headed towards midship. She slowed as they passed an open storage box. She peered inside.

The box contained lifejackets and other survival gear. She paused. If the yacht was in danger of sinking, they should grab lifejackets as a precaution. She reached into the box and froze as a glint of metal caught her eye.

She pushed aside the top life jacket and stared at a gun. It rested atop a pile of life jackets. She knew next to nothing about guns, other than the fact that they had one true purpose: to kill people. She rearranged the life jackets to get a closer look. She was careful not to touch the gun.

Was it Raphael's gun, or did it belong to the yacht's owner? It was an odd place to store a weapon. Most people kept their weapons on their person, or at least in private quarters under lock and key. She had no idea if most mariners even carried weapons, but many probably carried protection when they traveled to remote places. But only a fool would toss their gun in an unlocked storage box on deck.

A fool or someone ready to use it.

She bent to get a better look at the gun. She had no idea whether or not the firearm was loaded, or how to check. Jace and Uncle Harry probably knew no more than she did. She considered her options. She could remove it for safety, but that might alert Raphael. If she left the weapon, though, Raphael could use it against them.

Of course, Raphael might be unaware of the items in the box since it wasn't even his yacht. However, since the storage box was open, he had almost certainly placed the gun there, or knew about it.

She glanced up towards the men, who were by now thirty feet away. She turned back to the storage box and rearranged the lifejackets from one side to the other to get a better look at the contents. A coiled rope rested at the bottom of the box. That didn't alarm her, until she saw the other items.

A cry caught in her throat when she saw the hatchet, chainsaw, and a box of latex gloves.

"Kat?" Jace beckoned for her to follow. "Come on."

She waved him ahead. She had to remove the gun and hatchet, but had nowhere to hide them. The safest place was her stateroom, but they had planned to stay together. Leaving now might jeopardize their safety.

"Kat, hurry." Jace stood at the door.

She grabbed the hatchet and shoved it under a lounge seat cushion. She would return for it later. She shoved the gun barrel into the waistband of her jeans like she had seen in the movies. She just hoped like hell it wouldn't fire. She had no idea if the gun was loaded, or even how to tell whether the safety was on. She walked stiffly in Jace's direction, petrified the gun might accidentally discharge.

Jace frowned as he held open the door. "We're supposed to stick together."

Kat nodded and dropped her gaze to her waist. As Jace's eyes locked on hers, she lifted her shirt and showed him the gun tucked into her waistband.

"What the hell, Kat?" He stared at the gun. "You could get us killed."

A few whispered words were woefully inadequate to explain how she had morphed into the equivalent of a pirate, so she didn't try. She focused instead on the task at hand: incapacitating at least one desperate man and seizing control of a ship that didn't belong to her.

At least Jace knew she had the gun, though he didn't know that it might not be loaded. Raphael knew, so using it as a threat was risky. She followed behind Jace as they entered the passageway that led to the ship's engine room. Raphael and Uncle Harry waited inside.

"We've got to divide and conquer. The ship's sprung a leak, and the bilge pump is broken." Raphael pointed at Kat and Harry. "You two, check the engine room and stop the water from going in. Jace and I will try to seal off the hull."

She hesitated, but they could hardly refuse Raphael's instruction if the ship really had taken on water. "The ship's been anchored here the whole time. How on earth did it suddenly spring a leak?" Most vessels this size were double-hulled to prevent this exact situation. Even she knew that. The odds of a bilge pump failure were equally slim.

"We'll figure that out later," Raphael said. "Every second we waste talking makes it worse. Get in there and start bailing."

She followed her uncle through the door into the engine room. It was cleaner than she expected but windowless. Harsh florescent lighting shone down and glinted off the floor. It was slick with water.

However the water got there, she had to cooperate. Doing anything different than bailing out a sinking ship would raise obvious alarm bells to Raphael. She decided against pulling out the gun. Since she didn't know how to use it, it would almost certainly be disastrous.

"I can't tell where the water's coming from." She scanned the area for a bucket or something to scoop the water with but found nothing. A bucket was impractical in the first place, since there was just an inch or so of water on the floor. She turned to Uncle Harry. "We should be bailing out the bilge, not the engine room."

There wasn't even anywhere to empty the water. Raphael had separated them so he could get Jace out of the picture, she realized. He would return for her and Uncle Harry next. Her heart pounded as she realized she hadn't seen Gia for over an hour. If the situation was so dire, why had Raphael left her asleep in her stateroom?

Out of Raphael's sight, she could at least show her uncle the gun. He might even know how to use it.

As luck had it, he did. "Where did you get this?" He checked the safety, then opened the chamber. He turned the gun over in his hand. "It's loaded."

She recounted her find amongst the lifejackets. "You sure you can shoot this if you have to?"

"It's been a while, but it's like riding a bicycle. Not something you easily forget." He turned it over in his hand and handed it back to her.

"No, you keep it. We might need to use it." She waved her hand away. "It'll be easier for you to hide it."

"You calling me fat?" Uncle Harry patted his stomach. "I gotta eat like everyone else."

"Of course not. It's just that your vest has so many pockets, Raphael won't notice."

"True." He unzipped his vest and placed the gun into an inside pocket. "I haven't pulled a trigger in decades."

The water level rose to a couple of inches. Alarming, but hardly a catastrophe. "I doubt there's a leak here. The water's so low. Maybe something got spilled instead." Either way, it was odd that the expensive yacht lacked a backup system. Maybe something had been switched off by accident.

Uncle Harry looked around for something to scoop the water with. "I don't see the problem either. This ship can handle a little water."

They couldn't hear the men's voices outside, just a steady drip of water. "It's hardly the emergency Raphael made it out to be."

"He just sent us on a wild goose chase." Uncle Harry turned towards the entrance. "Let's go find Jace."

Kat grabbed her uncle's arm. "Wait. We need a plan first."

The sound of metal on metal screeched from somewhere above, followed by a loud bang.

Uncle Harry's hands flew to his ears. "What was that?"

The water drip had increased to a steady flow, like a tap had been turned on. It seeped into the hold from above them, not below. "He's flooding the engine room with water. Let's go!"

She raced to the door and grabbed the handle. She turned it, but it didn't budge.

The water rose quickly and now reached her shins. The engine room was probably watertight. If it was, they would drown within minutes unless they found and stopped the source of the water.

She jumped as a loud bang echoed against the walls. The lights blacked out and the engine cut. The power had been cut.

A killer was on the loose and they were powerless to stop him.

Chapter 36

The water reached Kat's thigh and continued to rise. She ran her palm over the wall of the hold, feeling for a way out in the darkness. She had searched the entire surface twice over in the last fifteen minutes. The only possible exit was through the locked door. "We've got to bust it open somehow."

"I'm trying," Uncle Harry's voice was hoarse from shouting. "I can't find anything to pry it open with."

Their banging and yelling yielded no response from anyone outside. That Jace hadn't come to get them out was extremely worrisome. He knew they were trapped inside and would have rescued them if he could. What had Raphael done to him?

"You've got the gun. Can you shoot out the door?"

"It's a metal door. You've been watching too many movies. That's not real life."

"Try it anyway. We've got no other options."

"Worth a shot, I guess." Uncle Harry pulled the gun from his vest pocket. "Here it goes."

He removed the safety, took aim, and fired. The bullet hit with a metallic clang and ricocheted off either the wall or the hatch before it splashed into the water. In the dim light it was impossible to tell if he had hit his target or not. The hatch door remained closed.

"How many shots do you have?"

"Dunno. It depends on the gun, and I'm no expert on the different types. And whether it was fully loaded in the first place. I didn't have time to check. Now it's too dark to see."

The water now reached her hipbone, and the dank air was harder to breathe. "We're not going to last in here. There's got to be a way out." Claustrophobia overcame her despite her refusal to think about it.

"I'll move closer to the door. That might work." Uncle Harry waded towards the hatch door.

"Careful, Uncle Harry."

"You know what's odd?"

"Besides us being caught in here?"

"The boat isn't listing," he said. "If she had taken on water, we would be tilted, but we're not. Yet the water's rising."

The water rise was alarming. They had another five minutes at most before the water reached the ceiling. "Maybe shoot upwards instead of the hatch door."

"We'll never escape that way."

"No, but somebody will hear us." A hole in the ceiling also bought them some time. Maybe it was wood instead of metal.

Uncle Harry shifted his stance and aimed for the ceiling. "Here goes."

The shot rang out before Kat had time to answer. It didn't ricochet or reverberate this time. The bullet must have lodged in the ceiling. She held out faint hope that it was wooden.

The gun clicked.

"That was the last bullet." Harry's voice held a note of desperation as he waded towards Kat. "I guess there were only two."

Bile rose in Kat's throat. They would die in here unless they drained the water. There was probably some way to do it, but neither she nor Uncle Harry knew enough about ships to even know where to look. She imagined a giant plug. If only it were that simple.

Suddenly the hatch door creaked open as a stream of light shone inside.

Kat breathed a sigh of relief. Jace had come for them.

A dark figure crouched by the door. "Get over here." Water spilled outside.

It wasn't Jace. It was Pete instead.

Kat waded towards him as fast as she could. Uncle Harry splashed a few feet behind her.

"Hurry, before Raphael gets here." Pete's face was flushed and he looked angry as he pulled Kat, and then Harry, from the flooded engine room.

Kat was relieved to see lights. The power had been cut only to the engine room, not the entire ship.

"Thank goodness you came for us. You saved our lives." Kat squinted as she stumbled through the doorway. Her heart skipped a beat as she saw Jace. His face was bloodied and his shirt was torn. He stood behind Pete.

A cry caught in her throat as she rushed towards him and wrapped her arms around him.

He pulled her tighter and kissed her.

"We've got to shut off the water." She shivered. "Where's the shutoff?"

"Already taken care of." Pete motioned them towards the deck. "Let's get out of here."

"Raphael knows that his secret's exposed." Jace grabbed her arm and steadied her. His nose was bloodied and his shirt was ripped. "We don't have a lot of time."

"What happened, Jace?" Harry asked. "Raphael did that to you?"

"He tried to shove me in the hold, but I got him back." He shook his head. "I grabbed him but he got away. I think he's going to set the yacht on fire. We've got to stop him before it's too late."

Pete held up his hand in protest. "Count me and the crew out. We're leaving. You should too."

"You can't just leave and let him get away with murder," Kat said. "We need to take him down."

"Do what you want, but we're outta here." Pete turned and headed to the stairs.

"Do the right thing and help us, Pete. We just have to hold him till the police arrive."

"Uh-uh." Pete looked back as he climbed the stairs. "Me and the guys aren't talking to the cops. See ya."

It suddenly dawned on Kat that Pete and the crew had probably all been in trouble with the law before. Who else would willingly crew a stolen boat? "Okay, fine. We won't call the police until you're gone. But at least help us tie him up."

Pete paused.

"He's already killed two people, Pete. If any of us die…" She couldn't finish her sentence.

"Okay, but let's make it quick."

Jace pointed towards the stern. "He had a gasoline can. I think he was headed to the galley."

They emerged on deck and ran towards the galley. They passed four crew members who pointedly ignored them as they tossed their gear into the dinghy.

Pete paused for a moment, then fell in behind Uncle Harry. Kat trailed behind the men.

They reached the galley and found Raphael. Two large gasoline canisters sat on the counter. Raphael held a third one with both hands as he poured it on the floor.

"Put it down, Raphael." Jace strode towards him.

Pete remained motionless in the doorway.

Kat got a sick feeling that Pete wouldn't do a thing.

Raphael straightened and taunted Jace. "Just try and stop me." He raised the can and threw the can at Jace. The liquid splashed Jace's face and shirt.

Jace's hands flew to his face. "My eyes!"

Kat grabbed Jace and pulled him towards the sink. She turned the taps on full blast and cupped the water in her hands. She splashed it on Jace's face.

"Don't bother. He's going up in flames, just like you." Raphael lit a match and grinned. "Nice knowing you."

Chapter 37

Harry pointed the gun at Raphael. "Put that thing out."

"If you shoot me, I'll fall. So will the match." Raphael walked towards Harry and Pete. "Drop the gun and let me pass."

Harry backed up towards the door as Raphael advanced. "Take it easy."

Kat held Jace back as he tried to intervene. "You're covered in gasoline," she whispered. "You'll burn if you go near him."

Raphael was inches from Uncle Harry, the match still lit. He grabbed a sheaf of papers and lit them with the match. He shoved past the men with the burning paper in his hand. He grabbed the door and turned. Then he threw the burning papers backwards.

She braced herself for an explosion.

Nothing. The papers landed several inches short of the spilled gasoline. The flames turned to embers, and then burnt out.

Suddenly Raphael lurched forward and then fell to the ground.

"Nice work," Pete said.

Uncle Harry turned to Pete. "I never thought to trip him."

Raphael lay face first halfway out the door.

"I'll grab some rope to tie him up," Pete said.

"Wait!" Kat realized with alarm that if Raphael had one match, he probably had a book of matches somewhere in his pockets. "He's still got matches. Get him out on deck."

Pete grabbed Raphael's arms as he fought them. Harry grabbed his feet.

"Let me go, Kat. They need my help," Jace said.

"No, rinse the gasoline off first. I'll go." Kat ran over to the other men and grabbed one of Raphael's legs. "Let's get him in the hot tub." It was one way to get the matches wet.

Jace didn't heed her advice, which was a good thing, since Raphael fought them tooth and nail.

Fifteen minutes later the four of them collapsed in exhaustion. Raphael was imprisoned in the hot tub. His back was propped against the ledge so he wouldn't go under. His legs were bound with the rope from the storage chest, and his arms tied together in front with zip ties Pete had found somewhere on board. It had taken all of them to subdue a fighting Raphael. Or Frank, as it were.

"One spark and this thing's gonna blow. Let's get to the dinghy," Pete said.

Kat glanced up at the sky as thunder rumbled a few miles in the distance.

She had to convince Pete to stay aboard and not depart with the crew. She glanced over at the dinghy and couldn't believe her eyes.

The dinghy was gone.

She scanned the waters but it was nowhere in sight. The crew hadn't even waited for Pete. They were probably long gone even before the altercation with Raphael in the galley. Pete's choice had cost him.

Pete and everyone else noticed too. It was only natural, given that the dinghy was their only means of escape from a gasoline-soaked ship with a flooded hull. Would the crew alert authorities? Probably not.

Frank cursed and squirmed in the hot tub. "Untie me and I'll pay you. It'll be worth it, I promise."

Uncle Harry snorted. "You'll pay us with our own money? I don't think so."

"Where's Gia?" Kat spun around. "Has anyone checked her stateroom?" Gia's absence seemed like an eternity, and with Frank incapacitated, they could safely leave him for a moment. She motioned to her uncle. "Let's go get her." She paused. "Depending how sick she is, we might have to carry her upstairs."

They had no way of getting off the yacht, but at least they would be together.

Jace and Pete guarded Raphael. Kat and Uncle Harry headed below deck.

Chapter 38

Gia's stateroom was dark. Kat and Harry headed to the bed where they found Gia unconscious and unresponsive.

Kat pressed her ear to Gia's chest. If she was breathing at all, she couldn't hear anything, nor see the rise and fall of her chest. She shook her friend but got no response. Raphael must have drugged her martini. "Gia, wake up!"

Nothing.

Kat was about to start CPR when she felt a slight breath on her face. "Gia?" She shook her friend and was rewarded with a grunt.

Gia suddenly choked and gagged.

Kat cast a worried glance at her uncle as they lifted her to a sitting position. "She looks terrible."

Gia's eyes flew open. "I'm going to be sick. Help me to the bathroom."

Kat and Uncle Harry each supported an arm as they accompanied Gia to the head. They exchanged anxious glances. Kat held Gia's hair back as Gia retched over the toilet. They couldn't afford to wait, but they couldn't move Gia in her present condition.

A minute later they helped her to a chair. She rubbed her eyes. "My head is killing me. I can't remember what happened. I'm never drinking again."

Despite the gravity of the situation, Kat couldn't resist a little humor. "You always say that."

"Oh, I mean it this time." Gia groaned. "How much did I drink?"

"Just one martini."

"Just one?"

Kat nodded. "You were drugged."

Gia's eyes widened. "How's that possible? You don't think Raphael…"

"I don't think, I know. You remember the fake lettering on the boat? The passports?"

Gia nodded slowly. "That bastard spiked my drink?"

"Well, it certainly wasn't any of us," Uncle Harry said.

"Why would he do such a thing?"

"Tell you later," Kat said. "Right now we've got to get on deck and get you walking. You need to get that stuff out of your system."

"Can't we go later?" Gia leaned back on the bed. "I'm really tired. And dizzy."

"No, Gia." Harry tugged on her arm. "We have to go right now."

Luckily Gia was too tired to protest and did as she was told. "Lead the way."

Uncle Harry locked his arm in Gia's and walked her to the door behind Kat.

"Where is Raphael? I want to give him a piece of my mind." Gia's words were slurred, but she was gaining strength.

"That's exactly where we're going," Kat said. "If I were you, I wouldn't hold anything back."

Chapter 39

Frank's teeth chattered as he rubbed his zip-tied hands against the edge of the hot tub in an effort to cut them. Kat flipped the hot tub's power switch as she, Gia, and Uncle Harry circled their chairs around Frank. The cool water hampered his futile efforts. It was like watching a caged animal when you knew how the story would end. Kat felt a pang of guilt until she remembered the full extent of Frank's crimes.

Pete had gone to the bridge to radio the police.

Gia was still groggy from the martini, but she listened quietly as Kat and Uncle Harry recounted the events of the last hour. Her eyes grew wide and she became more alert with each new revelation of Frank's deeds.

Jace reemerged on deck. He had changed out of his gasoline-soaked clothes and brought dry clothes for Kat and Uncle Harry, too. Kat couldn't break away for even a split second to change. She couldn't let Frank out of her sight.

The clouds had moved in low and close, and the sky was almost as dark as night. The thunder and lightning had shifted several miles south as day turned to evening. It had also started to rain.

Uncle Harry turned on the bar's transistor radio and turned up the volume. The radio blasted an AC/DC tune, but it competed with static from the poor radio reception.

"Shut that crap off," Frank said.

"What? Can't hear you." Uncle Harry stretched the power cord and carried the radio over to the hot tub and held it above Frank. "Hey, the reception's better over here."

Frank's eyes widened in panic. "Get that thing away from me. You'll electrocute me."

Uncle Harry swung the radio back and forth above Frank. "I still can't hear you."

Gia stood and swayed slightly. "I think we've forgotten something, Frank." She glared down at him as he thrashed helplessly in the water.

"What?"

"You've already got a wife, don't you?" Gia motioned to Harry to bring the radio closer. The electrical cord's slack disappeared as he stretched the cord. He held the radio above Raphael. Alanis Morissette belted out "Jagged Little Pill". "Or should I say, had one."

The color drained from Frank's face. "I don't know what you're talking about. Put the radio down, Harry."

Harry placed the radio on the deck, but Gia immediately picked it up.

"You don't know what I'm talking about? C'mon Frank, I know who you are. Frank Bukowski's no billionaire. He's not even a good husband. Raphael Amore is nothing more than one big fat lie. I'm not falling for any more of your crap. I want my money back."

"It's too late." Raphael fixated on the radio as Gia brought it closer. "The money's already gone. You'll never get it back."

"Maybe you'll never get out of that hot tub."

Kat exchanged glances with Jace. Gia was a woman scorned. A woman with a temper.

The final notes of "Jagged Little Pill" played as Gia brought the radio within inches of the hot tub.

"Gia, don't!" Raphael pleaded. "I'll get you the money, I promise. Just put that thing down!"

Gia snapped her fingers. "Got a pen, Harry? I need you to write some stuff down. Kat, grab your laptop. We're getting my money back now."

Moments later Kat returned, in dry clothes and with her laptop. She sat at the bar and waited for her computer to power up. Her prayers were answered as she got a weak Internet connection. After what seemed like an eternity, she navigated to the website of the first Costa Rican bank and entered the password Frank had provided. "Uh-oh, Gia. It says password invalid."

"Don't hold out on me, Frank." Gia fastened two zip ties around the radio handle. She made a daisy chain from the remaining zip ties and slipped them onto the end of a broom handle. Now she could hold the radio inches above the waterline and be insulated from the electric shock if it made contact.

The radio dangled precariously above Frank, like a baited fishing rod. The radio disc jockey announced an intro to Adele's "Turning Tables".

"I can't think straight with you holding the radio above me. Set it down."

"No, Frank." Gia shook her head. "I think the radio's highly motivating." She swung the radio back and forth in an arc above him. Adele's voice faded and strengthened with each pass. "It's kind of hypnotic, too."

"Stop it!" Tears rolled down Frank's face. "I'll tell you. Just don't kill me."

"I feel sorry for you, Frank. I really do." Gia spoke softly. "Too bad you didn't give Melinda and Emily a last chance. Did they plead for their lives too?"

"They deserved what they got."

"A four year old, Frank? How could you be so callous?" Gia slipped on the deck and almost lost her balance.

"Careful!" Frank's voice rose in pitch. "You'll kill me if you drop that thing."

"Melinda and Emily deserved to die, but you deserve to live? How does that work, Frank?" Gia lowered the radio until it swayed a few inches above his head.

"Stop it." Tears streamed down Frank's face. "What do you want from me?"

"The bank passwords, for one thing."

Frank rattled off a new password, a combination of letters and numbers.

Harry scribbled on his notepad, adding it to the long list of bank accounts and passwords.

Kat entered the password and pressed enter. "I'm in." She scanned the transactions. They had all started two weeks ago, which meant Gia was almost certainly the defrauded victim. She whistled at the amount.

"Three hundred thousand? That's your investment?"

Gia nodded. "Most of it is from mortgaging my salon. Can you get it back?"

Kat studied the transaction details. "I think so." She entered a new transaction, the mirror opposite of the original one. "Are these your account details?"

Gia nodded.

Kat held her breath and pressed enter.

"It worked?"

Kat nodded

"Hey! That's my money," Frank shouted. "Give it back."

"Uh-uh," Harry said. "I want my money back too. Where is my check?"

Frank told him and Jace disappeared inside.

Gia clapped her hands, almost sending the radio into the water. "At least I got my money back."

"No, we don't know that yet," Kat said. "It's still the weekend, so the transaction might get rejected when the banks open on Monday. No way to know for sure until then."

Gia turned to Frank. "It never was your money, Frank."

Frank's teeth chattered. "C-can I get out of this thing?"

"Uh-uh." Gia relished her newfound control over Frank. "Not for the moment, anyways. You're not going anywhere until we rip up Jace and Harry's checks."

Jace returned a few minutes later with his and Uncle Harry's checks. He handed one to Harry and tore his check into little pieces. "That's a relief. I guess we're back where we started."

"Not quite," Kat was relieved that Jace had actually written a check rather than transferring the funds. With the checks destroyed, everything was restored to normal. Money-wise at least. "Frank here murdered his family, and we've got to see justice served. Where's Pete?" He hadn't returned from inside.

"He's long gone." Jace pointed to the island. "The dinghy was already gone, but I saw him in the water. I think he swam to shore."

Chapter 40

It was almost midnight by the time the Coast Guard responded to their flares. The coast guard transferred them off the yacht and onto their ship. They hauled Frank off first and locked him up somewhere onboard. He still shivered from the hot tub, which proved a very effective way to quiet him.

Frank refused to speak to their rescuers, other than to demand a lawyer.

The coast guard vessel returned to the Victoria harbor and was met by the police, who boarded the vessel and removed Frank in handcuffs. They all watched as he was led into a waiting police van. His brilliant smile had morphed into a scowl, and his designer clothes had been replaced by borrowed track pants and a grease-stained t-shirt.

"Can't say I'll miss him," Jace said. "I'll be covering his trial though. You think he'll be convicted?"

"I'm sure of it. The surveillance cameras recorded his whole confession." Kat had hoped they were operational, and the police had just confirmed it. "That should be all the evidence they need."

"Who brings the yacht back to Vancouver?" Harry stared wistfully out to the sea. "I'd love to sail on it again."

"Catalyst belongs in Friday Harbor, not Vancouver. It was stolen, remember?" The yacht needed repairs after Frank's destruction, and the owner had to be contacted. Once evidence was collected, arrangements would be made for its safe return.

"Maybe one day I'll be rich enough to buy it."

Jace laughed. "Don't count on it, Harry. Besides, money's not everything."

"It sure isn't," Harry agreed. "At least I got to marry someone. Kind of a shame things didn't work out."

"It was a wedding to remember." Gia patted his arm. "Things will work out just fine. I'm sure of it."

They spent the next few hours at the police station where they provided further details of their ordeal. Raphael had clammed up, but his recorded confession and evidence gathered by Kat and the others was enough for multiple charges. In addition to fraud charges, he faced first-degree murder charges in the deaths of Anne Melinda Bukowski and Emily Bukowski.

In addition, he faced charges in Washington for the theft of the yacht.

"I almost forgot." Kat handed a small box to the police officer. It contained Melinda's wallet, Frank's passports, airline tickets, and the fake engagement rings. "You'll need these."

"For fools and traitors, nothing." Jace smiled.

"Brother XII might have got his gold, but Frank sure didn't," Kat said.

Uncle Harry arched his brows. "Huh?"

"History just repeated itself, Harry. Only this time, with a happy ending. This time, the thief hadn't gotten away." Further details of Frank's crime would no doubt emerge in the coming weeks, but Kat had already pieced most of it together.

After Frank killed his wife and daughter, he had headed south on a second boat he had hidden nearby. He sailed through the Gulf Islands and crossed the border from Canada into the United States. He had arrived at Friday Harbor in the San Juan Islands within hours of sending Melinda and Emily to their watery graves.

He laid low there for a few weeks, sleeping aboard his boat and watching for a boat that was unattended. That's when he noticed the Catalyst. The boat was unoccupied and wouldn't be missed. He hired Pete and the others, wharf rats who asked no questions and wanted none in return.

He painted over Catalyst's name with *The Financier* and steered clear of police. As long as he didn't stay anywhere long, no one questioned his presence on the yacht.

His Bellissima Blowout scam was dreamt up when he walked into Gia's downtown salon. She was simply the first woman gullible enough to fall for his charms.

The rest was history.

It had been a long weekend, even though it was only Saturday night. Kat couldn't wait to get to the hotel they had booked overnight. They would return to Vancouver tomorrow, and she wouldn't be leaving again any time soon.

"You got a good story, Jace?" Harry clamped a hand on Jace's shoulder.

"Oh boy, do I ever." Jace smiled. "A treasure trove of stories."

Chapter 41

Three weeks had passed since Raphael's arrest, but it seemed like yesterday. They had decided to celebrate Gia's close call with an end-of-summer barbeque. A chill hung in the air as the sun sank low on the horizon. Kat pulled her shawl around her shoulders. She always looked forward to autumn as a time of new beginnings and fresh starts. No one deserved one more than Gia. She was just grateful that her friend had gotten a second chance.

Jace and Harry manned the barbeque, while Kat and Gia sat at the patio table and nursed their margaritas. Their house was a big step down from *The Financier*, but at least they came by it honestly.

"A toast." Kat clinked her glass against Gia's. "We're safe and sound, and so is our money."

"Thank goodness," Gia said. "I'm so glad you talked some sense into me. I didn't want to believe it, but in the end you were right. Raphael—I mean Frank—really was just after my money."

"I wish things hadn't turned out the way they did. It must have felt like a fairy tale."

Gia stared wistfully off in the distance. "It was like a dream. How did I manage to get so brainwashed? I know…drop dead gorgeous, smart, and rich too. He just made me feel so special, Kat. Like I was a movie star or something. It's bittersweet, but in my heart I knew he was too good for someone like me."

"That's where you're wrong, Gia. You were too good for him." The gate latch clicked and they both turned. Pete beamed and waved hello as he headed towards Jace and Uncle Harry at the barbeque.

"Now there's someone else who deserves a new start," Gia said. "Just think, if you weren't lost in that cave, we wouldn't have gotten to know Pete."

Kat nodded. "Sometimes people aren't who they appear to be." Pete was a case in point. He was just someone who had lost his way and lost hope.

Pete had abandoned ship, but he hadn't forgotten them. His fear of police stemmed from previous run-ins years ago when he was homeless. He had spent a few decades doing odd jobs, whatever work he could get. Uncle Harry had found him a place to stay nearby, in a small walk-up apartment. He had a job as caretaker and handyman, in exchange for free rent.

"Next time I'll listen to you before I give all my money to some guy I just met. I can't believe you got it back," Gia said.

Kat waved her hand in dismissal. "I just typed a few keystrokes. You and the radio made all the difference."

Gia laughed. "I can't actually believe I did that. The drugs must have still been in my system."

"You seemed pretty focused to me," Kat said. "I'm just glad everything worked out in the end."

"Hard to believe I fell for it." Gia sipped her drink. "Everything about that guy was just a façade, with other people's money. I still can't believe he murdered his family. And to think I could have been next." Gia stroked her neck absent-mindedly. "Do you really think he would have killed me, Kat?"

"Sooner or later."

"That sounds so flippant."

"Of course he would. He killed Melinda after a four-year marriage. You meant nothing to him."

Gia sucked in her breath "Really, Kat? You should work on your bluntness."

"People like that have no feelings for anyone but themselves. Frank was a cold-hearted, cold-blooded killer. My words might be harsh, but it's good to face the truth." Melinda's wallet was the key that unlocked Frank's deception. It surprised Kat that he had even kept it. He probably saw it more as a trophy than anything else, since there wasn't a sentimental bone in his body.

"Some girls have all the luck." Gia twirled her hair in her fingers as she sat opposite Kat. "Me, not so much."

"I have to disagree," Kat said. "You've got a wonderful life. Look at everything you've got."

Gia smiled. "And to think I almost lost it all because of that jerk."

The men joined them at the table with platefuls of steaks and baked potatoes.

Uncle Harry spooned coleslaw onto his plate and turned to Pete. "Why were you hanging around the Friday Harbor marina if you don't work on boats?"

"I never said I didn't work on boats," Pete said. "Just that I didn't crew."

Harry frowned.

"I do custom millwork, carpentry, that kind of stuff. I hang around the marina and word gets around." He paused. "I work cheap."

"I think I can get you some more work. If you want it, that is." Gia turned to Kat. "I'm glad you got my money back. I've got another investment lined up."

"Gia, don't do it. You and I have the worst luck." Uncle Harry rose and headed back to the barbeque.

"Not that kind of investment, Harry. I'm renovating my salon. The best investment I can make is in myself, and I think Pete here can help me."

"I can take a look tomorrow." Pete chewed a mouthful of steak. "All good." Kat turned to Gia. "I'm glad everything's okay now."

"Almost everything," Gia said. "Except that I'm still married to that jerk."

"Maybe, maybe not," Kat said.

Gia brightened. "What do you mean, maybe not?"

"I called a lawyer friend. Your case is a bit complicated, but basically Raphael couldn't marry you since he's already married to someone else."

Gia gasped. "But they weren't married anymore. I mean, she was…dead."

"Poor Melinda. It's true that she had already passed before your wedding ceremony."

"Then I don't see how…"

"A death certificate hadn't been issued yet. As a widower, he wasn't free to marry anyone else until that certificate was issued. That meant your marriage wasn't legal in the first place." She flashed back to the news reports and shuddered to think that Gia might have suffered the same fate. "Aside from that, the marriage license was issued to Raphael, not Frank. The marriage isn't valid because of his misrepresentation."

Gia beamed. "I'm not married after all?"

"That's right. You don't have to get annulled or divorced or anything like that."

"Told you I was lucky," Gia said.

"You call that lucky?" Kat laughed. "Too bad you weren't lucky enough to avoid him in the first place."

"I've learned my lesson. I won't trust every hot-looking guy, and I won't be marrying one, either. At least not any time soon."

"What's this about getting married?" Uncle Harry returned to his seat with a second steak. "I'm available for wedding ceremonies later this month."

"Relax, Harry," Gia said. "I am not tying the knot. I've decided I don't need a man at any cost. They're kind of an expensive habit."

"You're doing great on your own," Kat agreed. "That's the reason Raphael targeted you in the first place."

"And next time, I call the shots." Gia giggled. "I want a man who wants me for me, not for my money."

"I'm glad to see you've come to your senses," Harry interjected. "I knew the guy was trouble from the first moment I saw him."

Kat raised her brows. "Is that so?"

"Yep. But there's nothing wrong with tying the knot. I hoped to convince another couple."

"You mean Kat and Jace?" Gia turned to Kat. "Why not? We can have the ceremony right here. We can go dress shopping tomorrow."

Harry rubbed his hands together. "I'll wear my tux. First time in twenty years. I hope it still fits."

Jace smiled at Kat. "We're getting hitched?"

"Can I straighten your hair?" Gia turned to Kat. "I've got a new product I want to try on you."

"Over my dead body." Kat ran her hand through her hair. "I like my hair just the way it is."

She turned to her uncle and smiled. "I promise you'll be the first to know when we do tie the knot." She and Jace weren't purposely keeping their plans a secret, but they weren't ready to share them yet, either. Timing was everything, and sometimes the best plans were no plans at all.

Did you love Blowout? Get the other books in the series and Colleen's other books. Visit her website to sign up for twice yearly new release notifications: http://www.colleencross.com

Author's Note

This is a work of fiction, but with some fascinating historical facts woven in. The historical figures in my story are all but forgotten today, but history always repeats, and this story is no different.

The best thing about writing fiction is that you can make stuff up. The second best thing is researching facts and imagining a first-hand experience. So what is fact and what is fiction?

Raphael and Gia's story is pure fiction, although similar deceptions in love and money occur all the time. I wish they didn't, but they do. Pete is also purely fictional and is not Brother XII's descendant.

Brother XII is fact. He was a real person, and the story is mostly fact with just a few fictional twists thrown in. His real name was Arthur Edward Wilson. West coast sailors traveling along Canada's Pacific Coast will recognize the Brother XII name and be familiar with Pirates Cove, De Courcy Island, and Valdes Island.

Brother XII (his preferred spelling, not mine) established the Aquarian Foundation at Cedar-by-the-Sea on Vancouver Island near Nanaimo, British Columbia in the 1920s. Brother XII and his notorious cult were famous worldwide for their Armageddon predictions in the 1920s and 1930s, yet today they are largely forgotten.

When his cult attracted too much scrutiny, he and his followers moved offshore to the much smaller Valdez and De Courcy Islands. I've focused the story mostly on De Courcy Island, rather than the multiple locations for simplicity. I've also changed the geography, topography, and cave locations to fit the modern day story.

Charismatic people like Brother XII appear with surprising regularity throughout history. Every few years they trick gullible people with belief systems, combining cult of personality, mysticism, and religion. They capitalize on our desire to be part of something larger than ourselves. Too often it has tragic results.

The buried gold in the Mason jars is fact according to corroborated accounts from the 1920s. Whether it still lays buried is another story. Although the estimated half-ton of gold coins was too heavy for Brother XII to take with him on his trawler, it's very unlikely the gold stores remained untouched and hidden over the decade or so that his cult was active. I also doubt it remains on the island, though the myth persists. More likely he depleted the gold stores gradually over the years and took whatever remained when he left De Courcy Island for good in 1933.

Or maybe I'm wrong and some lucky person will discover the gold treasure. At a thousand dollars an ounce, it would be worth more than fifteen million dollars today.

The undersea passage between two islands is fact. In my story it connects De Courcy and Valdes Islands. In reality, the undersea tunnel connects the Valdes Island cave to Thetis Island, not De Courcy. The subterranean passage is two hundred feet below the cave entrances. The passage was well-known and used by local Coast Salish First Nations people for ceremonial initiation rites for at least hundreds, and probably thousands, of years, until a late nineteenth-century earthquake rendered it impassable. It would have been blocked in Brother XII's day, too. But if it wasn't, I suspect he would have hidden his gold coins there.

And you already know Kat, Jace, and Harry are fiction. They exist only in my imagination but they are very real to me!

I hope you enjoyed reading Blowout, the third book in the Katerina Carter Fraud Thriller series and the sixth Katerina Carter story overall. You can check out the related Katerina Carter Color of Money series for more. As long as readers like you enjoy my stories, I will continue to write them. If you loved Blowout, get my other books. See www.colleencross.com for retailer links. You can stay up to date on my latest releases by signing up for my twice-yearly newsletter at www.colleencross.com

Also By Colleen Cross

Katerina Carter Fraud Thriller Series

Exit Strategy

Game Theory

Blowout

Katerina Carter Color of Mystery Series

Red Handed

Blue Moon

Greenwash

Nonfiction

Anatomy of a Ponzi: Scams Past and Present